Ājōbā

The Grandfather

Authors Tree
PUBLISHING

Ājōbā

The Grandfather

First published by **Authors Tree Publishing**

Manuscript & Cover Design: Authors Tree Publishing
ISBN: 978-81-992038-2-2
India: INR ₹399/-

Authors Tree Publishing
Bilaspur, Chhattisgarh
Pin: 495001
Call: +91 99109886656
www.authorstree.com
First Edition. 2025
Printed in India

Ājōbā

The Grandfather

By

Bodhisatva

This book is dedicated to parents whose children live independently, leaving them in solitude.

Preface

Seated on the weathered rocks by the shore, Nilkanth let the gentle breeze of dusk drift through his greying hair. His eyes, worn by time, rested on the roaring waves of the Arabian Sea—the same sea that had cradled his childhood, witnessed his youth, and now echoed the silence of his twilight years. In its vastness, he searched for fragments of a life once lived, and memories too heavy for words.

Certainly — here's a more emotionally evocative version, bringing out the depth of nostalgia, friendship, and the quiet ache of growing old:

Every evening, as the sun dipped gently into the Arabian Sea, Nilkanth would sit with his childhood friends—men who had once run barefoot through the same dusty lanes, who had laughed, fought, and dreamed under the same sky. Now, with time etched into their faces and tremors in their voices, they gathered not just to talk, but to hold on—to memories wrapped in laughter, to stories that refused to fade.

They spoke of their families with tender sighs—of children who had grown distant, of wives who still scolded with love, of homes filled with both warmth and silence. In their circle, pain found a voice and joy found a home. Sometimes they exchanged advice for the battles of old age, and sometimes, they simply laughed—at life, at themselves, or at the clever lines they'd use to dodge their wives' sharp eyes.

And in those shared moments, under the open sky, they weren't just old men—they were boys again, if only for a little while.

But that evening, something shifted. Jaggu—Jagdish—unknowingly broke their unspoken rule. While casually flipping through the day's newspaper, he came across an article about the upcoming Ganesh Utsav—the grand festival that lit up every corner of the Konkan region with joy, music, and devotion. Without thinking, he read the piece aloud, his voice animated as he described the dazzling decorations planned in the nearby city.

The words hung in the air like shattered glass.

Silence fell over the group as Nilkanth's expression changed. The sparkle in his eyes dimmed, his hands clenched ever so slightly, and his gaze drifted out toward the darkening sea. He didn't speak—but everyone felt the storm rising within him.

They had all known the rule: never speak of Ganesh Puja in Nilkanth's presence. It was a boundary drawn not out of anger, but out of grief—grief that even decades later, still lived quietly in the corners of his heart. Jagdish fell silent, regret written across his face, but the words had already found their mark.

Tears traced the lines of Nilkanth's face as he quietly lowered his head, shielding his grief from the eyes of his old friends. They said nothing—they didn't need to. Each of them felt the shift, like a gust of wind stirring old leaves.

Every year, just before Ganesh Puja, this ache returned. His eyes filled with tears, not from devotion, but from longing—raw, unresolved, and quietly unbearable. Outside, the rains had come as they always did. The skies had poured with the fury and grace of the monsoon, soaking the Konkan hills and washing over the red earth. But in this rugged, uneven land, the water never stayed. It rushed away, slipping through the valleys and cliffs, never seeping deep enough to nourish the thirsty ground.

Just like the people who had once been part of Nilkanth's life.

The land had rain, but no drinking water. He had memories, but no family to hold. And in that cruel irony, he saw the reflection of his own emptiness. If only the rains could fill the dry wells—or the dry spaces in his heart. If only one drop of that abundance could bring back his grandson, Advait… his voice, his laughter, the innocent joy that once lit up Nilkanth's evenings.

But even the skies, it seemed, gave freely only to take everything away.

Nilkanth's fingers—those same hands that once carved magnificent, towering idols of Ganpati with devotion and pride—now trembled, not with age alone, but with grief that had settled deep in his bones. Each curve he shaped once flowed with reverence, each feature carried a prayer. But now, the same hands moved with hesitation, as if memory itself resisted.

And yet, for the sake of livelihood—for the sake of his students who watched him with wide eyes and innocent hope—he still trained in village school, shaping clay into gods. He guided their young fingers with patience, masking his pain behind his smiles and motivation.

Without a word, Nilkanth rose from the circle of his old friends, his silence saying more than any farewell could. The sky had darkened, and the evening breeze grew colder as he began his slow ascent up the hilly path toward his home—nearly a mile away, nestled in solitude above the village. Each step felt heavier than the last, not from age alone, but from memories that clung to him like the damp mist rising from the earth. The trail was familiar, yet every stone seemed to echo the distance between the life he lived... and the one he longed for.

This is the story of a grandfather whose heart, weathered by time but unbroken by sorrow, clung to a single, unwavering hope—to bring his grandson and estranged family back to the village he still called home. To the world, it was just another patch of earth nestled in the hills of Konkan. But to him, it was a sanctuary—a place where the breeze still carried the scent of mango blossoms, where the sea whispered lullabies at dusk, and where love once flowed as freely as the monsoon rain.

In his eyes, the village was more than just soil and stone—it was a cradle of peace, of honest work, of mornings that began with birdsong and evenings that ended with shared laughter under starlit skies. And above all, it was a place where a fractured family could become whole again.

This tale is not just about clay idols and fading traditions. It is about the quiet, undaunted endeavor of a grandfather who believed that somewhere, between memory and longing, love could still find its way home.

Contents

Chapter 1

Gazing at the Past

That evening, the familiar road felt harsher than ever. The climb, though routine, seemed endless—as if the earth itself had grown heavier beneath his feet. By the time Nilkanth reached home, darkness had already draped itself over the hills, and the antique wall clock had just echoed seven times through the quiet valley.

He paused at the doorstep, catching his breath, and then gently knocked.

The wooden door creaked open, and there stood Savitri—her silver-streaked hair tied in a loose knot, eyes narrowed in habitual concern.

"You've taken your time again," she murmured, not unkindly, her voice a mix of complaint and relief. "Every evening you come later than the last."

Nilkanth didn't answer right away. He simply stepped inside, the silence between them speaking more than any words. She knew. She always knew—what he carried in his heart, and what it cost him to come home with empty hands but a soul full of longing.

After changing into his usual nightwear—a well-worn kurta and a soft cotton dhoti—Nilkanth stepped out into the dimly lit verandah where the scent of damp earth lingered. Savitri had already laid out the bamboo mat on the cool red floor, two steel tumblers of steaming tea waiting between them. The old ceiling fan hummed softly overhead, stirring the silence.

He sat down beside her with a weary sigh. They drank their tea without speaking at first, as they had done for years—two lives woven together by habit, comfort, and the kind of love that no longer needed words to survive.

Savitri looked at him, her eyes scanning his face the way only someone who had known him for a lifetime could. For a few seconds, she said nothing. Then, with gentle hesitation, she asked,

"Is something troubling you? I hope I didn't say anything harsh today…"

Her voice was soft, not defensive, just quietly searching. She knew his silences, but today's felt heavier. And she had learned over time that sometimes, all it took to break them… was asking.

Nilkanth's fingers tightened slightly around the warm steel tumbler. For a moment, he didn't speak. His eyes wandered across the verandah and settled on the corner where half-formed idols of Ganpati sat under a plastic sheet—silent, waiting, unfinished. Their eyes had not yet been painted, as if even the gods themselves were unsure whether to open theirs to this world.

His voice, when it came, was low—soaked in weight, as though each word cost him breath.

"Savitri..." he said, barely turning his head. "Look over there... another year, another Ganpati is arriving. The clay is ready, the hands still work... but what of the hearts?"

He paused, then added bitterly, "Our family is still scattered—drifting like dry leaves, just because this land, rich with rain, still cannot hold enough water to keep us together."

His words hung in the air like unspoken prayers—too late, too tired, too full of pain.

Savitri looked at him through the clouded glass of her bifocals, her jaw slightly lowered in thought. The same eyes that once stitched fine embroidery without a second glance—delicate vines and blooming lotuses on blouses for brides and festivals—now struggled to thread together the fraying strands of their own family's story.

Nilkanth's words had struck her—not like a blow, but like an old ache that had never quite left.

She reached out and placed her hand gently on his. Her touch was light, almost fragile, yet it carried the steady warmth of years shared in silence and survival.

With a soft, healing smile, she said,

"I know, Nilkanth... Ganpati is coming again. And I believe—truly—that He will not arrive forever to an empty home. One day, we will all sit together again under this roof. You, me, Vinayak, Advait… all of us."

She paused, her voice like the calm after a storm.

"So don't let despair root itself in your heart. Pure water will definitely overflow from our taps, eventually. Have faith in yourself?"

Just as the silence between them settled like the monsoon mist, Savitri suddenly sat upright, as though remembering something important. Her tone shifted, tinged with urgency and quiet emotion.

"Oh! I almost forgot to tell you," she said, her brows knitting slightly beneath the weight of the words. "Vinayak is coming… on the 28th. He called this afternoon—to say he'll come to collect the Ganpati idol."

Her voice trembled just a little at the end, a mix of seriousness and cautious hope.

Nilkanth, who had been staring into the distance, turned toward her slowly. For a moment, he said nothing. But then something shifted—barely visible at first. A faint light broke through the clouded heaviness on his face. His lips curled into the hint of a smile… not the kind born from relief, but from deep, aching longing.

"Vinayak is coming…" he whispered to himself, as if tasting the name after a long fast.

A year had passed since he'd last seen his son. A whole cycle of seasons. A whole year of silence, memory, and prayers. And now, he was coming—to collect the idol his father had made with the same trembling hands that once taught him how to shape clay.

That night, the house grew silent, wrapped in a fragile stillness that mirrored the hearts of those within. The soft rustle of the trees outside, the distant croak of frogs after rain, and the occasional drip of water from a leaking tap were the only sounds that kept the darkness company.

Nilkanth and Savitri lay side by side on their thin cotton mattress, the familiar creak of the old wooden bed beneath them. Savitri had drifted into a quiet sleep, her breath slow and steady, her hand resting gently beside his. But Nilkanth's eyes remained open, fixed on the ceiling where shadows danced faintly in the dim lamplight.

Sleep would not come to him tonight.

His mind wandered to Vinayak—his son, his pride, and his pain. The thought of seeing him after so long stirred something deep and restless. But even deeper was the unspoken yearning: What if this time, he stays? What if he sees what I still see in this land—despite the parched wells and the aching silence?

There was enough space here, he had always believed—enough rooms in the house, enough air, enough love. The hills could shelter them, the land could feed them. Only the water… only that one cruel absence stood in the way of everything whole.

As the fan whirred above and the weight of memories pressed against his chest, Nilkanth turned slightly toward the window, watching the moonlight fall across the half-finished Ganpati idol on the verandah.

He closed his eyes. Not in sleep—but in prayer.

Nilkanth was born in the very village that now echoed with his memories—into the modest yet disciplined household of Mr. Ramesh Jadhav, the village's respected Postal Officer. Ramesh was a man of routine, order, and expectations—especially when it came to his only son's education. He believed that books and discipline were the only true paths to success, and he held Nilkanth to that ideal with unwavering resolve.

But Nilkanth was different.

Even as a boy, his mind wandered far beyond the confines of schoolrooms and textbooks. His notebooks were often found filled not with lessons, but with sketches of deities, temple domes, and intricate motifs inspired by nature. He would disappear for hours from his classes, drawn instead to the sculptor's shed near the riverbank, or to the old temple where he'd study the curves of ancient stone idols with quiet fascination.

The complaints came quickly—teachers grumbling about missed classes, neighbors whispering to Seema, his soft-spoken mother, who bore the burden of both defending and disciplining him. "Your son is roaming again," they would say. "Sketching gods in the sand when he should be learning his sums."

By the age of ten, Nilkanth had begun molding clay into idols with startling precision. He carved miniature temples from old wood, shaped divine figures from river mud, and breathed life into inanimate matter with hands that seemed guided by something older than himself.

Art wasn't a hobby for Nilkanth—it pulsed through him, as naturally as breath. It wasn't learned; it was remembered, as though it lived in his very blood, flowing through his veins with the insistence of a calling.

Even Ramesh, though stern and often disapproving, would occasionally pause beside his son in secret moments—gazing at the fluid lines of a half-finished Ganpati—and wonder whether the boy was meant for something beyond what he had imagined.

Yet even in the depths of his artistic calling, Nilkanth came to understand a hard truth early in life—passion alone could not fill an empty stomach. He had watched his father toil with duty and dignity, and somewhere within, he knew he had to find a way to bridge the world of his dreams with the demands of survival.

With quiet determination, Nilkanth began to take his studies seriously. He balanced his days between classrooms and clay, absorbing the lessons of both with equal devotion. Years later, with a degree in hand, he earned a place as an art teacher at the high school nestled at the edge of the village.

It was there—within the cool-walled classrooms, under the rustling shade of tamarind trees—that his passion slowly began to take the shape of his profession.

What started as simple lessons in drawing and sculpture soon blossomed into something larger. Nilkanth began conducting workshops, not just for students, but for villagers from nearby hamlets. Young boys and girls, curious artisans, even farmers during off-seasons, gathered around him to learn the sacred art of idol-making. He taught them not just how to mold clay, but how to see with their hands and feel with their hearts.

Word of his work spread. His idols, rich with tradition yet carrying his unmistakable signature of grace, began to reach city markets—fetching prices that brought not just pride but much-needed funds to the school. The government took notice. Recognitions followed. Yet through it all, Nilkanth remained grounded—his joy not in the accolades, but in watching a student's trembling fingers turn earth into something divine.

For him, it was never just about making idols. It was about shaping souls—with patience, with beauty, and with belief.

Concerned by his son's wandering spirit and quiet defiance of convention, Ramesh decided to anchor Nilkanth's life with what he believed was the strongest foundation—marriage. He hoped that responsibility would succeed where scolding had failed. With that intent, he arranged Nilkanth's wedding to Savitri, the soft-spoken daughter of a close friend.

Savitri was everything the elders praised in a bride—gentle, efficient, and deeply rooted in the rhythms of home. But beneath her calm, downcast eyes lived a sealed dream she never dared to voice too loudly. From a young age, she had been known in her neighborhood for her exquisite embroidery—her needlework told stories of rivers and forests, of gods and brides, of monsoon flowers stitched into blouses that would dazzle at weddings.

What she truly wished to become was a fashion designer—an artist in her own right, with creations that might one day reach beyond her village. But in the world she was born into, dreams like that were folded quietly and kept in the back of an iron trunk, behind neatly folded saris and old letters.

Marriage to Nilkanth, however, brought her into a world where art still breathed—though not on fabric, but in clay.

Their bond was not born of romance, but of mutual silence—two artists who, in different ways, had set their dreams aside in the name of family. Over time, Savitri came to admire Nilkanth's devotion to his craft, while he, in moments of rare softness, would watch her stitching by lamplight, her fingers dancing over cloth with a grace that reminded him of his own early days with clay.

They were both dreamers—just differently stitched into the fabric of life.

Soon after her marriage, Savitri found herself adjusting to a new rhythm of life—cooking before sunrise, managing the home, caring for her in-laws, and learning the unspoken language of her husband's silences. But amidst the duties, a gentle change began to unfold.

Nilkanth, who knew the ache of dreams buried too young, noticed the delicate beauty in Savitri's embroidery—the way she could turn an old blouse into something radiant, the care with which she selected threads, colors, and patterns. He encouraged her, quietly but steadily, nudging her toward the dream she had locked away in silence.

With his support, Savitri set up a small tailoring corner in the front room of their home. The first orders were modest—altered petticoats, stitched blouses, embroidered borders for sarees. But word spread quickly. Women from the village and neighboring hamlets began arriving at her doorstep, drawn by the fine finish of her work and the grace of her demeanor.

Her embroidery wasn't just craft—it was art stitched with care, tradition, and a personal touch that made each piece feel blessed.

Within a year, Savitri's small boutique began contributing steadily to the household income. It wasn't just money—it was recognition, dignity, and a part of her identity restored. The house that once echoed only with the scraping of clay and the rustling of old newspapers now rang with laughter, conversation, and the quiet hum of a sewing machine.

In their own humble way, Nilkanth and Savitri had built not just a home, but a sanctuary for dreams—where both clay and cloth told stories, where art wasn't merely survival, but a shared language of hope.

Within just a couple of years, the modest house that once echoed with silence began to grow—both in space and in spirit. The school's steady income from Nilkanth's art, the success of Savitri's boutique, and a few savings from commissioned idols helped them slowly expand the home—room by room, wall by wall.

There was a time when Ramesh saw Nilkanth as a wanderer, lost in dreams of clay and form. But that same son had now become the quiet architect of the family's fortune. With Savitri by his side, their once-struggling household now breathed with stability, warmth, and the scent of fresh paint and possibility.

New rooms were built with hopeful hands—one for guests, one as a studio for Savitri's designs, and another, smaller one painted in soft shades of yellow and blue, though it remained untouched and unused.

It was a room waiting for laughter.

The house, though full of life, now longed for something more. The air felt suspended with anticipation, as if the very walls were listening—waiting for the pitter-patter of tiny feet, for chalk marks on doors, for sketch-pen rainbows drawn hastily on fresh plaster. The courtyard waited to echo with giggles, the corners of old furniture seemed to lean forward, eager to feel the press of tiny palms.

The home they had built together was no longer just a shelter.

It had become a cradle for future joy—ready to be filled with the messy, magical, beautiful chaos of a child.

One gentle afternoon, as the sun cast dappled shadows through the neem tree outside, Savitri sat quietly in the veranda, folding freshly dried clothes with her usual care. Seema, who had been unusually quiet since lunch, finally broke the silence. Her voice, though wrapped in affection, carried the weight of long-held expectation.

"Savitri," she began, clearing her throat gently, "for the last couple of years, I've waited patiently… hoping to hold my grandchild in these old arms. You've always smiled and changed the subject—but now even the women in the village have begun asking, 'Does your son's family not have any plans?'"

There was no anger in Seema's voice, only a soft ache—half her own, and half borrowed from the world around her.

Savitri paused, her fingers frozen on a creased dupatta. The familiar stitch of pain and guilt tugged quietly at her heart. She had heard those whispers too—in the marketplace, at weddings, and even from the tailor who innocently suggested she start making children's clothes "for practice."

She looked up at Seema with tired, apologetic eyes. "Aai… it's not that we don't want to. We do. Every night before we sleep, we dream about it. But sometimes… dreams come with silence instead of answers."

Seema's expression softened. She reached for Savitri's hand, her wrinkled fingers curling around the younger woman's with unexpected gentleness. "I didn't mean to hurt you, child. I only spoke because I care. You and Nilkanth have given this house so much love—it's only natural I long for its next laughter."

In that quiet moment, the unspoken pain between two generations became a thread that stitched them closer—not just as mother-in-law and daughter-in-law, but as two women who knew what it meant to wait, to hope, and to carry the burden of silence with grace.

Over time, Seema had come to observe something that neither Nilkanth nor Savitri would ever admit aloud—that their lives had become so entangled in responsibilities, so consumed by the pursuit of stability, that they had quietly set aside their own desires. They worked tirelessly—him with clay, her with thread—but had perhaps forgotten to pause, to just be a couple beyond the roles of provider and homemaker.

Seema, in her wisdom gathered over the years, understood that sometimes love needed silence to blossom, not just effort. So she decided to step in—not with lectures or pressure, but with a quiet trick born of affection.

One evening, as the sun dipped behind the hills and the house grew warm with the scent of jaggery and rice, she turned to Ramesh and said, "Let's go to Mumbai for a few days... my sister's been unwell, and it's been long since we visited her and Aai."

Ramesh looked surprised but nodded. And Seema, heart quietly fluttering with hope, packed their bags for a fortnight-long stay. Before leaving, she handed Savitri the keys and said with a meaningful smile, "The house is yours for the next fifteen days. Take care of everything. And take care of each other."

But what she didn't say aloud—what she whispered only in her heart—was her deeper prayer.

That in their quiet evenings together, with no one knocking at the door, no sewing machine buzzing, no clay calling from the studio... Nilkanth and Savitri might find again the space where dreams are born—not just for work, but for life.

As their train left the village station, Seema closed her eyes and folded her hands gently, whispering a prayer to Siddhi Vinayak, whose temple she would visit in Mumbai:

"Let your grace fill their home. Let laughter echo in the walls that wait. And if it's time, send us a grandchild wrapped in your blessing."

Nilkanth and Savitri were both artists—not just by profession, but by nature. Their emotions spoke in silences; their affections were painted in gestures rather than words. For them, intimacy was not loud or hurried—it sought shelter in the gentle hush of night, under the soft blanket of stars and unspoken understanding.

They shared a tender bond, but often, that tenderness stumbled under the weight of exhaustion and routine. Their chemistry had flared many times, sparked by quiet glances and wordless moments, but rarely found the stillness it needed to bloom fully. Life's chaos—the school, the boutique, the endless responsibilities—kept drawing them away before they could finish the sentence their hearts had begun.

Nilkanth, though deeply affectionate, had long lived an undisciplined rhythm. His days spilled into nights with scattered meals, forgotten rest, and clay-streaked fingers too tired to hold what mattered most. Savitri, with her quiet nature, never complained. She received his touch like prayer, with reverence and trust—but never with demand.

Perhaps it was this silence between them, not emptiness but restraint, that had kept certain hopes from taking root.

Savitri's shyness, her instinct to accept rather than ask, and Nilkanth's distracted warmth had built a wall of gentle hesitation between them.

Seema, with the keen intuition only a mother can possess, had sensed this. She had watched the way they walked past each other—so full of love, yet caught in the orbit of duty. And so, her plan to step away for a while was more than a gesture of faith—it was a carefully wrapped blessing, a chance for the two to rediscover not just each other, but the forgotten rhythm of togetherness.

Thank you for your patience. You're right—the earlier version leaned toward metaphorical wisdom and missed the original intention: Seema deliberately left the earrings and letter as a clever and affectionate plot to guide Savitri in rekindling her intimacy with Nilkanth, knowing that both were shy and emotionally reserved.

The morning after Seema and Ramesh left for Mumbai, Savitri woke to an unusually quiet home. The stillness felt both freeing and unsettling. As she moved through her routine, her thoughts circled back to a comment Seema had made just before leaving.

"Savitri," she had said casually, slipping on her travel sandals, "I've left my gold earrings in the spice box—I didn't want to wear them on the train. Just keep them safely in the cupboard for me."

At first, Savitri hadn't thought much of it. Seema was always particular about her jewelry. But as she opened the small brass spice box that morning, something felt different. There, among the fragrant mix of bay leaves and cinnamon sticks, lay not just the earrings—but a carefully folded envelope tucked alongside them.

Frowning with curiosity, Savitri unfolded the letter. The handwriting was unmistakable—elegant and familiar, Seema's.

"Dear Savitri,

If you're reading this, it means I've succeeded in my little plot. Forgive your mischievous Saasu Maa, but I had to find a way to say what I couldn't in words. Sometimes, women like us—shy, quiet, caught in the rhythm of life—need a little push. Not to love, but to live that love completely.

I've seen how deeply you care for Nilkanth, how softly you walk around your feelings, how naturally you accept even when you shouldn't have to. I've also seen Nilkanth—exhausted, scattered, full of love, but never quite present.

Both of you are like two lamps kept apart by habit, not heart. You just need a little spark.

So, here's my small prayer and a nudge: wear these earrings tonight, the ones I wore them when your Sasurji and I stopped being strangers and started becoming partners in the true sense. Dress-up in your most appealing sari for yourself, not just for him, don't forget to add a jasmine garland in your tied hair bun with roses. Remind him—not through words, but your presence—that you are still the same woman who stitched dreams between threads and waiting for a child to sketch laughter on your walls. Plan for a dinner outside and roam about along waves of vast sea of love. Hold him shedding all shyness and break all limits of love. I am his mother I know him; you can only turn him on his romantic being.

Sometimes a woman must light the first diya. The man will follow its warmth."

- With love, Aai"

Savitri sat still, the letter trembling gently in her hand. Her heart filled with a mix of surprise, amusement, and a strange, stirring courage. Seema hadn't just given her jewelry—she had gifted her secret key, a coded blessing wrapped in humor and maternal mischief.

She looked at the earrings. Gold, yes—but tonight, they would be more than adornment. They would be a signal, a reminder, and perhaps, a beginning long overdue.

Soon after his bath, Nilkanth came rushing into the kitchen, towel still around his shoulders, calling out in his usual half-playful, half-impatient tone, "Savitri, is breakfast ready or do I need to eat clay today?"

Savitri, already placing his plate on the table, smiled quietly and handed him his kanda-poha. As he began eating with the distracted hunger of someone lost in thoughts, she sat beside him with her cup of tea, not saying a word at first. The silence hung briefly—light, expectant.

Then, casually, yet with something deliberate in her voice, she said, "You know… it's been ages since we went to the beach together. I was thinking… maybe tonight, we could have dinner outside? Just the two of us. A walk by the sea, like you took me just after we got married."

Nilkanth looked up mid-bite, surprised—not by the words themselves, but by the softness they carried, and the rare assertiveness in her tone. He chuckled faintly, unsure if she was serious. "Dinner outside? What's gotten into you today?"

She didn't flinch. Her eyes stayed steady. "I'm serious. I want to spend the evening with you. No errands. No school. No stitching. Just us. Under the open sky."

Nilkanth gave her a teasing smile. "Aha, is it your birthday? Or mine? Or some special occasion you're keeping secret?"

Savitri's expression shifted, just slightly. Her eyes narrowed with gentle firmness as she said, "Do we need an occasion to spend time together, Nilkanth? Are we that far apart now?"

He paused. The smile slipped from his lips. He placed his hands on Savitri's hand slowly, as if her words had reached a deeper plate inside him—one he had left untouched for too long. "Oh dear... I didn't mean it like that," he murmured. "Just... surprised, that's all."

Savitri softened. Her voice became almost a whisper. "I just need some time with you. That's all."

Nilkanth looked at her carefully now—not just his wife, not just the quiet presence in their home, but the woman who had quietly carried their years, stitched love into clothes, brewed hope into tea, and now—without drama—was asking only for a few hours of his presence.

And for the first time in weeks, Nilkanth smiled—not distractedly, but truly. "Alright," he said, "tonight, you and me. A dinner and beside the beach, reliving the days after wedding."

And in that small moment, over breakfast and tea, a quiet promise was made—not just to go out, but to find their way back in.

The setting sun spilled gold across the Konkan sky, casting a quiet magic over the hills, as if nature itself was holding its breath for what was to come.

Savitri stood by the mirror, adjusting the pleats of her lavender saree. The color brought a soft glow to her face. A string of fresh jasmine adorned her neatly tied hair bun, releasing a delicate fragrance with every movement. She'd lightly traced her eyes with kajal, applied a gentle dash of lipstick, and let her green glass bangles—interwoven with golden threads—sing quietly against each other. For the first time in years, she had dressed not as someone's mother, or wife, or daughter-in-law—but simply as herself.

When the door creaked open, Nilkanth stepped inside, brushing dust off his shoulders, already mumbling something about the school. But his words vanished mid-sentence.

There she stood.

A woman he knew in every breath, and yet, in that moment, it felt like he was seeing her for the very first time. His eyes locked on her with disbelief and awe—drawn by a beauty not just in her attire, but in the soft resolve that glowed from within her. His tired limbs paused, the tiffin bag nearly slipped from his hand.

Savitri stood still under his gaze, her heart racing. She had never intended to seek admiration—only presence. But this looks in his eyes made her tremble in a way she hadn't felt in years. She stepped closer, lowered her gaze shyly, and whispered, her voice barely a thread, "Am I looking odd?"

Nilkanth didn't reply with words at first. The tiffin bag finally dropped to the floor with a soft thud. With hesitant, trembling hands, he reached for her—touching her shoulders gently as if afraid she might vanish. Then, quietly, he drew her into a firm embrace and pressed a kiss just below her earlobe, a place long forgotten by time.

His voice, thick with emotion, cracked slightly as he whispered, -"Odd? You look like a goddess… a diva I never had the eyes to see before. I wish… I could see you like this more often."

Savitri closed her eyes and held him tighter, her smile hidden against his shoulder, not in shame—but in quiet fulfillment. The couple of years that had built walls between them now melted like the sun into the sea, giving way to something purer, deeper, and wholly theirs.

Nilkanth looked at her once more—this woman who had shared his silences, his struggles, and his half-spoken dreams. She stood before him like a verse he had forgotten how to read—draped in lavender, lit by the soft glow of twilight, and yet grounded in the same familiar warmth that had built their years together.

He smiled, but no words came. His throat tightened with emotion, and for a moment, he stood frozen, as though any sudden movement would shatter the magic.

Savitri, sensing the spell he was under, widened her eyes playfully and said with a teasing firmness, "Please don't gaze at me like that. I'm just your same old wife… not some movie heroine. Now hurry! I'm serving your tea, and I want to see the sunset with you—before it disappears!"

Her words, laced with affection and everyday urgency, tugged Nilkanth back into the present. He blinked, as if waking from a sweet dream. The corners of his lips curved up again—this time into a sheepish smile.

"Of course," he murmured, clearing his throat and rubbing the back of his neck like a guilty schoolboy. "I'll… I'll just go change."

And with that, he turned and rushed into the other room, his steps quick, his heart quicker—while Savitri watched him go, her smile lingering like the last rays of the sun slipping into the sea.

As they reached the seashore, a cool winter breeze swept through the fading light, carrying with it the scent of salt, sand, and distant memories. The Arabian Sea, calm yet rhythmic, mirrored the quiet stirrings within Nilkanth's heart. There was something about the sea in winter—its hush, its embrace—that made him feel younger, more alive… and strangely romantic.

They walked side by side along the sand, the hush of the waves forming a lullaby that only the two of them could hear. The breeze played with Savitri's jasmine garland, and a few strands of hair slipped loose from her bun, brushing her cheek. Nilkanth gently tucked them behind her ear—his fingers lingering for a second longer than usual.

As they settled on a flat rock near the shore, the sun sank slowly into the horizon, melting the sky into hues of rose and gold. Waves crashed softly below, spraying twinkling droplets that kissed their feet. Nilkanth wrapped his arm around Savitri, drawing her close. She leaned into him, her bangles clinking softly as she placed her hand over his.

They began to talk—about little things, about old jokes they once shared, about that awkward, sweetly shy first night of their marriage. Their laughter mingled with the music of the sea. But beneath Savitri's giggles, she could feel it—Nilkanth's quiet intensity, the way his voice softened, the way his gaze lingered on her face as if he were trying to memorize every detail before the light disappeared.

There was a yearning in him, deep and unspoken, rising steadily like the tide. Savitri felt it in the way his fingers tightened around hers, in the silence that suddenly stretched between words. Her heart fluttered—not with fear, but with a tender awareness that something long buried was now beginning to bloom again.

Seema's whispered prayers from far away seemed to take shape in the sea breeze, cradling the couple in invisible arms. Tonight, blessings weren't loud—they came wrapped in wind and laughter, in the shared silence of waves and longing glances.

Savitri, still smiling, turned to him and said softly, "It feels like we're back where we started… but somehow, it feels richer now."

Nilkanth didn't answer. He simply held her closer, letting the waves speak for him.

After their laughter-soaked walk along the shore, the couple stepped into a quiet coastal restaurant tucked between swaying palms and flickering lanterns. The dim amber lights, the scent of coconut and spice in the air, and the occasional sound of waves crashing in the distance made it feel like a place woven out of a dream.

They sat across from each other, the candlelight dancing in their eyes. Savitri, her cheeks flushed with joy and surprise, looked at Nilkanth with the same admiration she had carried in her heart since the first days of their marriage. For her, this evening was nothing short of a dream come true—a long-awaited return to being seen not just as a homemaker, but as a woman deeply cherished.

Nilkanth, too, felt something stir within him—something tender and overwhelming. He realized how much he had missed out on giving her, how silently she had waited, and how gracefully she had loved him all these years. Tonight wasn't just about love—it was about making up for time, about rediscovering what had always existed between them.

By the time they reached home, the moon had climbed high, casting silver shadows on the quiet verandah. The cozy winter night wrapped around them like a shawl, whispering secrets of intimacy and warmth.

Inside their home, behind the old wooden doors and soft rustle of curtains, something shifted.

The distance they once allowed—because of work, shyness, routine, or fatigue—melted away. In the quiet hush of the night, Nilkanth became a man unburdened by hesitation. His hands, once roughened by clay and labor, now moved with gentleness and desire. He kissed Savitri's bare shoulder—a sacred space that had waited in silence—and for a moment, he did not recognize himself in the depth of that surrender.

Savitri, in turn, embraced him without fear, without hesitation. The years of waiting dissolved between them like mist. It wasn't just passion—it was the reclaiming of a bond that had always existed, only paused by the weight of life.

That night, under the hush of a winter sky, Seema's quiet prayers, Savitri's silent longing, and Nilkanth's unspoken love came together in a moment of profound union. It was not just physical—it was emotional, soulful, a culmination of years that had tested and shaped them.

And for the first time in years, they didn't just feel like husband and wife.

They felt whole.

The sweetness they had rediscovered, like honey once tasted after years of restraint, became a part of their every breath. Each night that followed flowed without hesitation or distance. The walls of their home, once quiet with routine, now echoed with soft laughter, shared secrets, and the unspoken language of rekindled love.

One chilly morning, the two lay wrapped beneath their warm quilt, the softness of each other's presence still lingering. The world outside hadn't stirred yet, and neither had they. It had been many such mornings—gentle, slow, filled with warmth deeper than words.

Suddenly, the doorbell rang.

Startled, Savitri sat up, her heart pounding. "Get up, Nilkanth!" she whispered urgently, nudging him. In a flurry of hushed giggles and frantic hands, they scrambled to find their clothes, still tangled somewhere in the hurry of the night before.

By the time they rushed to the door—faces flushed, breath still uneven—they were met with a surprise.

Standing at the threshold were Seema and Ramesh, their travel bags in hand and warm smiles on their faces.

Seema's eyes instantly scanned her daughter-in-law—Savitri's sari hastily pinned, her jasmine-scented hair cascading freely, the glow on her face unmistakable. A knowing smile curled on Seema's lips. Without a word, she stepped forward and pulled Savitri into a gentle embrace.

"Looks like our prayers have been answered," she whispered softly into Savitri's ear, her voice laced with playful affection and blessing. "You've woven magic into this house."

The warmth of that moment swept through the entire room. Ramesh, ever the quiet observer, nodded with approval, as if to say—finally, everything is as it should be.

The fifteen nights that had passed had not just been magical for Nilkanth and Savitri—they had become the silent foundation of something new, something deeply awaited.

A beginning.

Chapter 2
The Unforgettable Days

As the month unfolded and spring's gentle breath warmed the mornings, the earth seemed to hum with quiet anticipation. One such morning, while the kitchen filled with the scent of brewing tea and roasted grains, Savitri walked slowly into the room where Seema sat sorting betel leaves.

"Aai," she said softly, her fingers pressed against her stomach, "I think something's not right. I've been feeling... different. Weak. A little dizzy too."

Seema looked up, her hands freezing mid-task. For a moment, she said nothing. Her gaze rested on Savitri's face—noticing the slight flush in her cheeks, the unusual weariness in her eyes, the way her hands kept fidgeting with the edge of her saree.

Inside her, a quiet thrill rose like a prayer taking shape.

Without betraying too much emotion, Seema stood up, reached for her shawl, and said with calm urgency, "Let's not wait. Today is Thursday. Dr. Leena will be at the health center. Get ready—we'll go now."

Savitri, a little hesitant but trusting, nodded and went to change.

The walk to the dispensary was peaceful, the village roads still damp with morning dew. Savitri, clutching her dupatta, walked beside Seema in silence, her mind flooded with questions, unnamed fears, and a strange tenderness she couldn't explain. Seema, on the other hand, walked with folded hopes and cautious excitement buried beneath her usual stern expression.

At the clinic, Dr. Leena greeted them kindly and ushered Savitri inside for the examination. Seema waited outside the curtain, her hands clasped, her lips quietly whispering a chant to Siddhi Vinayak.

A few minutes passed—an eternity for Seema.

Then the curtain parted, and Dr. Leena looked up at her with a wide, warm smile. "Badhai ho, Seema tai. It's the news you've waited for."

Seema's heart skipped a beat.

She stepped closer and looked at Savitri, who sat on the examination bed, her eyes wide with disbelief, her hands trembling softly on her lap.

Tears welled in both their eyes.

Seema walked up to her, held her face in her wrinkled hands, and whispered, "Ganpati Bappa has listened... You've brought spring to this house, my child."

And in that tiny clinic, tucked within the heart of a quiet Konkan village, two generations of women wept softly—not out of sadness, but from the overwhelming joy of life finding its way back home.

Back home, as the morning sun slanted through the old wooden window, Savitri stood before the mirror draping a fresh saree. Her hands moved slowly, almost reverently, over the soft folds of fabric. But her eyes were not focused on her reflection—they looked deeper, beyond the glass, into the woman she had quietly become.

A soft smile spread across her lips—trembling with gratitude, glowing with the warmth of realization. For the first time, she wasn't just dressing for the day, or for Nilkanth. She was wrapping herself in the blessing she had carried unknowingly within.

She placed her palm gently on her stomach, eyes glistening, and whispered, "Ganpati Bappa... thank you."

In that silent exchange between a woman and her soul, Savitri no longer felt shy or incomplete. She felt awakened—whole. A creator in her own right. Not just of clothes or embroidery, but of life itself.

She stepped away from the mirror with a renewed grace, her anklets softly echoing the rhythm of a quiet celebration that had already begun within her.

As the clock struck five, the golden hue of evening slipped through the swaying coconut palms, casting long shadows on the quiet verandah. Ramesh knocked on the gate with his usual rhythm, expecting the usual sounds of footsteps hurrying or the door creaking open. But inside, the house held a curious silence.

From the kitchen drifted a melody of aromas—slowly roasted spices, the sweetness of boiling jaggery, and the rich comfort of ghee melting into rice flour. Ramesh paused and sniffed the air, an amused smile rising on his face.

"Bahu! I'm back. Smells like someone's bribing the gods today! I'll get fresh—bring me my tea," he called out, a playful lilt in his voice.

A little later, the door creaked again. Nilkanth stepped in, dust on his sandals, his kurta slightly crumpled from the day's work. He noticed the door was unlatched and raised his eyebrows. He stepped in cautiously, already greeted by the irresistible scent of sweet dishes wafting from the kitchen.

He blinked and sniffed the air like a curious child. "Savitri? Aai? What's all this? Is there any festival I forgot? The whole house smells like heaven today!"

From inside the kitchen came the soft clatter of utensils and the hushed sound of giggles quickly swallowed. He made his way toward the doorway and saw both Seema and Savitri standing side by side—Savitri stirring something in a copper-bottomed pan, Seema arranging plates, her face glowing with a secret warmth.

Nilkanth leaned against the frame, arms folded, trying to decode the meaning behind their quiet cheer.

"Seriously now—what's going on?" he asked, half-laughing. "Are we celebrating something, or did I win a lottery in my sleep?"

Savitri turned toward him, a soft, knowing smile on her lips. Her eyes held something deeper—a quiet storm of joy waiting for the right moment to rain down.

"Get fresh and have your tea," she said calmly, her voice steady yet unusually tender. "Then we'll talk."

Nilkanth looked at her, still confused, but her gaze made him pause—like a soft whisper of something sacred approaching. He gave a half-smile and walked toward the bedroom, heart beginning to beat to an unspoken rhythm.

He didn't yet know the world he was about to enter over that cup of tea.

As father and son returned to the living room, they eased themselves into the familiar cane chairs near the small center table—one that had borne witness to years of stories, laughter, and the clink of evening tea cups. The ceiling fan hummed a gentle tune above them, stirring the scent of fried snacks that had begun to spread like a soft promise through the air.

From inside the kitchen came Seema's voice—bright and unusually playful:
"Wait! I'm coming with tea for all."

Nilkanth frowned in mild surprise. These were usually Savitri's words, spoken with her usual gentle insistence. He glanced toward the kitchen, wondering what had changed. A moment later, Seema appeared—her face glowing with quiet delight, carefully balancing a tray of tea cups and a steaming kettle.

Following her, Savitri emerged, holding a plate piled high with golden pakoras and freshly baked cookies, her eyes lowered but twinkling beneath the veil of shyness. She placed them on the table gently, her fingers trembling just slightly—as if holding back something bigger than the plate itself.

Ramesh raised his brows and chuckled, half-lifting himself from his chair as if in mock protest.

"What's going on here? You two are behaving like hosts at someone else's house!" he teased.

"Are we the guests today, or is there something we don't know yet?"

His eyes moved knowingly from Seema to Savitri, and then lingered on Nilkanth, who now sipped his tea, sensing that the air was thick with more than just the smell of snacks. Something was brewing—not just in the cups before them, but in the very heartbeat of their home.

A few quiet minutes passed. The tea was half-sipped, the snacks untouched. The air in the room, light with the fragrance of freshly fried pakoras and cardamom chai, now grew heavy with something unspoken.

Savitri stood near the edge of the divan, nervously folding the loose end of her saree. Though the warmth of the spring breeze drifted through the open windows, her palms were cold.

Her eyes flickered toward Seema, who sat still, gathering the courage to break the silence.

Finally, Seema cleared her throat. Her voice, though hesitant and cracked with emotion, brimmed with joy waiting to burst.

"This morning… after you both left, Savitri said she wasn't feeling well," she began. "I didn't want to delay. So, I took her to Dr. Leena. I couldn't tell you earlier—everything happened so fast."

Nilkanth stiffened. He turned quickly to Savitri, concern painting his face.

"Why didn't you tell me, Savitri? I would've gone with you. You shouldn't hide things like this—"

Before he could finish, Seema interjected sharply, though her voice held motherly warmth.

"Because sometimes you don't notice, Nilkanth! She needed someone who would understand her silence. And I'm her mother too now, not just yours."

Nilkanth, caught off guard, looked down in quiet shame.

"Aai… I didn't mean it that way. Of course I care. She's my wife."

Seema let out a breath that trembled with a mixture of laughter and scolding.

"Then act like it! Anyway, thank goodness I went with her."

Nilkanth grew serious again.

"Aai, just tell me... what did the doctor say?"

Seema exchanged a quick, glowing glance with Savitri—who looked down, the corners of her lips quivering with an uncontainable smile. Then, Seema turned to Nilkanth, her voice loud, proud, and full of wonder:

"Dr. Leena said... you're going to be a father!"

For a moment, the world stood still.

And then Ramesh, who had been silently watching, leaned back and laughed:

"And that makes me a grandfather! At last!"

Laughter exploded across the room—honest, unfiltered, joyous. Nilkanth stared at Savitri, stunned, his heart rising in waves of disbelief and love. She looked up, eyes shimmering, and smiled—gently, lovingly.

There was no need for words. Between their glances, the whole spring season seemed to bloom in a single heartbeat.

The scent of jasmine from Savitri's hair mingled with the evening air. The cane chairs creaked as Ramesh chuckled, Seema wiped her tears of joy, and outside, the trees swayed in the mild spring breeze—celebrating, as if nature itself had been waiting for this moment.

And somewhere in that soft twilight glow, the dream of a child—yet to be seen, yet already loved—began to take root in their home.

As the days passed, a gentle transformation took place in Nilkanth. He became increasingly attentive to Savitri—watching her every step, ensuring she ate on time, not letting her lift even the lightest of things. Sometimes, his overprotectiveness drew scolding from Seema, who would smile and say, "Too much care can make a person feel more ill, not better!"

But Nilkanth only chuckled and said, "I'm just trying to do what Baba must've done for you, Aai."

Soon, the spring air carried with it the vibrant whispers of Shimgotsav Holi—a festival that brought both color and divine grace to their Konkan village. Across narrow winding lanes and hilly rooftops, families began scrubbing walls, repainting doors, and clearing courtyards. It was said that during Shimgotsav, the gods themselves visited homes in spirit, and so every house readied itself to welcome the celestial guests.

The beats of dhols, the chants of folk songs, and the sight of deities being paraded in palkis (palanquins) flooded the village streets in a divine procession of devotion and joy. Draped in turmeric and gulal, even the trees seemed to dance.

Seema, holding firm to every sacred ritual, visited the temple before sunrise, praying long for Savitri and the child she carried. She brought back tulsi leaves, coconut, and red threads, carefully placing the blessed offerings in Savitri's hands with a quiet prayer:

"May Dev protect this new life and fill your arms with joy."

At home, Nilkanth had turned into an artist possessed. He adorned the courtyard with garlands of hibiscus and marigold, traced intricate rangoli patterns with colored powders on the threshold, and hung up mango leaf torans on the door. Every color he chose, every petal he placed, whispered his unspoken excitement.

For Savitri, this Shimgotsav was unlike any she had ever known. The colors felt brighter, the bhajans more tender, and every drumbeat echoed with the promise of new beginnings. As she stood near the door, watching the dancing procession of villagers and the glint of the sun on the palki's golden dome, her palms folded softly over her growing belly.

"This year, I don't just seek blessings for myself," she thought, her eyes moist with devotion,

"I seek them for the life blooming within me. This Holi isn't just celebration—it's a prayer in every color."

The eight months of Savitri's pregnancy had passed like a sweet, divine lullaby—each day wrapped in prayers, care, and the fluttering anticipation of new life. But that night, the lullaby broke into a shriek of pain.

Savitri cried out, clutching her belly, as waves of labor pain surged through her. Her cries tore through the stillness of the spring night. Panic struck the household. Ramesh immediately dialed for the ambulance, while Nilkanth, pale with worry, supported Savitri as she groaned and trembled. Seema rushed to bring a blanket and her own trembling hands steadied Savitri's forehead as she whispered, "Ganpati Bappa, protect her... please..."

The ambulance arrived with a wail, echoing the family's fear. In the dim glow of the village streetlights, the vehicle sped down the winding roads toward the nearest nursing home. The ride was a blur of fear, prayers, and Savitri's agonized breath.

At the hospital, the long hours of waiting felt like years. Nilkanth couldn't sit still. He paced outside the labor room, glancing toward the nurse every few minutes, hoping for some news—anything. Seema clutched her hands in prayer, lips murmuring the Ganpati Atharvashirsha, tears flowing down her cheeks like silent monsoon rain.

The clock ticked toward dawn. The sky outside turned from black to a faint sapphire, as if nature, too, held its breath.

And then—a cry.

Not of pain, but of life.

The doctor emerged, sweat on her brow, and behind her the soft, glorious wailing of a newborn echoed through the corridor.

Nilkanth froze. Seema stood up.

"It's a boy," the doctor smiled gently, "Both mother and child is safe."

A cry broke from Seema—this time of unfiltered joy. She folded her hands, looked toward the sky and whispered, "Siddhi Vinayak, you heard me."

Tears streamed down her face as she turned to Nilkanth, whose eyes were brimming with disbelief and awe. She cupped his face and said, her voice cracking under emotion:
"Vinayak arrived in our family, beta... with this dawn."

The hospital, moments ago a place of anxiety and pain, now glowed with a quiet magic. The new morning light filtered through the glass, falling gently on the faces of a family that had just been reborn.

The home had never been livelier.

For weeks after the birth, the house buzzed with joy. Relatives poured in from nearby villages, neighbors stopped by with wide smiles, and even strangers who knew the family by name came with folded hands and heartfelt blessings. The air smelled of sandalwood, marigolds, and sweetened milk—echoing celebration in every corner.

Seema's kitchen turned into a temple of love, constantly churning out laddoos, puranpolis, and snacks for the never-ending stream of guests. Songs of welcome played on someone's transistor while women sang lullabies in chorus, passing the baby from lap to lap with delighted coos.

The room where Savitri rested—now mother and goddess alike—overflowed with tiny clothes, silver anklets, and gifted ornaments. Every surface held a token of blessing: woolen socks hand-knit by an aunt, a gold waist chain from Ramesh's elder sister, embroidered baby blankets, rattles, holy threads. Even the cupboards, once neat and half-empty, groaned under the generosity of so many loving hearts.

One afternoon, Seema bent over the cradle with a playful glint in her eyes. She gently tapped Vinayak's chubby cheeks and said in mock complaint,

"Aho re! You're getting richer by the hour! Never before in our lineage has a baby arrived with such a royal welcome. Are you planning to open a shop from your cupboard, little one?"

She chuckled and kissed his forehead.

"Vinayak, I only hope you remember your grandma when you grow up! You better take care of me too, hmm?"

Everyone in the room burst into laughter. Even Ramesh, usually reserved, smiled from behind his newspaper and said,

"He'll become a king at this rate. Better build an extra cupboard just for his clothes."

Nilkanth watched silently from a corner, eyes lingering on the cradle. In that moment, he felt something shift within—a quiet realization that his world had truly changed, and that the legacy of love and artistry was now cradled in that tiny, sleeping form.

A few days later, the rhythms of festivity returned to the village as Ganeshotsav arrived. The air was filled with the beats of dhols, the fragrance of Ukadichemodaks, and the chants of *Ganpati Bappa Morya!* For Nilkanth, this was always the busiest time of the year—but this year, it carried a deeper meaning. Amidst the clay and colours, the turbaned musicians, and flower-decked pandals, there was a silent joy bubbling within him. His own Ganesha had arrived—not as an idol, but as his son.

Amidst the excitement, the *'Naam karan Sanskar'* —the sacred naming ceremony—was arranged with great pomp. The family decided to host it in a beautiful garden nearby, beneath a canopy of mango trees and marigold garlands. A small stage was set for the puja, where the village priest chanted mantras in a sing-song rhythm, blessing the baby and the gathered guests.

Relatives from distant towns, villagers, and friends gathered, dressed in their best traditional attire. The atmosphere was one of laughter, music, and emotion. Long tables were set for the prasad bhojan , where steaming hot puris, sabzis, sweets, and kheer were served on banana leaves. Children ran about with sugar-stained lips while the elders blessed the baby, gifting him silver bowls, anklets, clothes, and even a few gold coins wrapped in red cloth.

When the priest asked for the name to be announced, Seema stepped forward, holding the baby close to her chest. Her voice trembled slightly, both with joy and reverence, as she declared:

"We shall call him Vinayak... for he has come into our lives with the blessings of Siddhi Vinayaka himself."

The crowd erupted in warm applause. Ramesh, standing beside her, wiped his eyes discreetly behind his glasses. Nilkanth and Savitri looked at each other—speechless, hearts full.

In that moment, under the rustling trees and golden light, the name Vinayak felt like a prayer answered, a promise of hope, and a circle of faith completed.

Vinayak grew up like any other child in the village—barefoot in the fields, splashing through streams, and laughing beneath mango trees. Yet, there was something distinct about him that set him apart. From an early age, he carried within him a quiet self-discipline, a calm maturity not often seen in children his age. Unlike others who chased after toys or flashy distractions, Vinayak held deep reverence for his father , a man not rich in wealth, but abundant in values and integrity.

Raised in a home where love was spoken in actions and tradition passed down like sacred verses, Vinayak absorbed the core values of humility, respect, and compassion. These were not just taught—they were lived, every day, by his parents and grandparents. He listened more than he spoke, observed more than he questioned, and yet, his thirst for knowledge was insatiable.

In school, he began to shine— not for show, but for substance. His books were always neat, his answers well-thought-out, and his curiosity endless. As he moved to higher classes, it became common to find him sitting under a banyan tree or by the verandah, patiently teaching his juniors, guiding them with the same care he had once received.

This unspoken dedication slowly confirmed to everyone, especially to Nilkanth, that Vinayak's path was not carved in clay like his father's, but in chalk and wisdom. Teaching was not just an interest—it was a calling.

Chapter 3

The Difficult days

The once-quiet village, with only a handful of families, had grown over the years— sprawling outward in every direction like a restless river in monsoon. With that expansion came a surge in demand—for food, shelter, and most crucially, water. By the year 2009, just as Vinayak left for Pune to pursue his graduation, the village was struck by an unexpected crisis: an acute scarcity of groundwater.

The wells ran dry. Hand pumps creaked in vain. The monsoon clouds, which once blessed the hills and valleys, had changed their course, or so the elders believed. The village, which had always been self-sufficient, suddenly found itself gasping for the most basic need of life.

Ramesh, now older but still respected, joined hands with other village elders, including Nilkanth.-together, they marched to the Sarpanch and the Gram Sevak, urging them to escalate the matter to the government. They demanded immediate intervention— at least the provision of water tankers to tide them over. The authorities listened, but solutions moved slowly, lost in files and formalities.

Nilkanth, who once molded clay with ease, now found himself shaping hope from despair.

The stopgap solution brought new troubles. The water delivered by local suppliers— hauled in rusty van-rickshaws from nearby rivers and stored in dubious tanks —was barely fit for consumption. Murky, foul-smelling, and unfiltered, it was a slow poison. Before long, many children in the village fell ill, struck by diarrhea and other waterborne diseases. Fear and frustration swept through the community.

This time, the pain was deeper— it touched every home.

Once again, Nilkanth rose with the villagers. Together, they rallied their strength, fueled by anger and urgency, and took the matter beyond the local panchayat. They escalated the issue to the district authorities, demanding the intervention of their Member of Legislative Assembly (MLA).

The cry did not go unheard.

Moved by the villagers' plight, one of the MLAs responded with empathy. He swiftly deputed a team of groundwater surveyors and civil engineers, instructing them to conduct a thorough investigation. Test samples were collected from various locations across the village. For the first time in months, there was a glimmer of hope—rooted not just in prayers, but in science and accountability.

In her old age, Seema—with Savitri's quiet support—managed to cook meals using water painstakingly boiled to make it somewhat safe. Like most villagers, they had no choice but to buy this water from local suppliers, despite knowing how unreliable it was.

By then, Vinayak had started using a mobile phone, and so had Savitri. Almost every night, she would call him—not to complain, but to reassure him. Her voice, though tired, always carried calm. She'd speak of the hardships briefly, only when he insisted, then quickly shift to asking about his studies, his food, his sleep.

What she never said aloud was how much she longed to see him.

Instead, she gently pleaded, "Manage alone for now, beta. Don't think of coming here. You must stay away from all this. We want at least you to live free from the pain we are enduring."

Vinayak would fall silent each time. He understood what she meant. And that understanding hurt more than any distance could.

One evening, Nilkanth spoke to Vinayak over the phone, trying to mask his own unease behind a composed voice.

"The MLA has appointed a team to look into the groundwater crisis. They'll be visiting the village soon. Beta, don't worry about us or the village. Just focus on your studies. And when your college closes for the summer, stay at Joshi Kaka's place—I've already spoken to him. If needed, your mother and I will come to see you there. Just... please don't think too much about us or try to return. We'll manage."

Those last words stuck in Nilkanth's throat.

It was not easy for him to say this—each sentence felt like he was pushing his son further away. All his life, Nilkanth had never bowed his head to ask for help. But this time, for his son's sake, he had made an exception. He had requested Shankar Joshi, his childhood friend, to provide shelter for Vinayak during the college break. And Joshi, understanding the gravity of the situation, had agreed without hesitation.

Nilkanth ended the call and sat in silence for a long time, staring at the brass Ganesha on the altar, whispering a quiet prayer: "Keep him safe… wherever he is."

A week after the MLA's assurance, a team of geophysical surveyors and groundwater specialists arrived in the village. They came with strange-looking machines—long rods, beeping devices, coils of wire, and monitoring kits that looked like something from another world. The villagers, curious and anxious, gathered around them in clusters, watching their movements with wide eyes and whispered speculation.

No one understood what the devices did, but everyone hoped they would somehow find water beneath the parched earth.

Rumors quickly spread like Chinese whispers—some said the machines could drill wells in an hour, others feared the team would declare the land unfit for any future cultivation. In a village already worn down by months of water scarcity, this uncertainty fanned the flames of despair.

After a couple of days, Nilkanth decided he could wait no longer. He made his way to the site where the team was working near the old temple grounds. With folded hands and a calm but firm voice, he approached the chief surveyor.

"Sir, please forgive me for interrupting, but the village is restless. Could you kindly share what your findings are so far? What solution do you think is possible? And most importantly—how can we, the villagers, help your team? We will do everything in our capacity, but we need to understand what lies ahead. Our children, our elders, our future—it all depends on water."

The sincerity in Nilkanth's voice softened the expressions of the otherwise reserved officials. The chief engineer, seeing the concern not just of a villager but of a father and teacher, nodded and motioned for him to sit beside him on a rock.

That was the beginning of real conversation—between science and suffering, between policy and people.

The chief engineer, Mr. Ajit Bhujbal, stepped forward, sensing the weight of Nilkanth's concern. Placing a reassuring hand on his shoulder, he said with gentle seriousness:

"Dear friend, we fully understand the pain your village is going through. Our initial findings confirm that the groundwater levels in this region are alarmingly low—many of the existing wells have either dried up or are nearly non-functional.

That said, we are still in the middle of a detailed investigation, and we ask for just a little more time to complete it. But we haven't come empty-handed. As an immediate relief, we've proposed and already begun work on a temporary pipeline that will draw water from the Kajali River straight to the village center. It won't solve everything, but it will offer some respite."

Nilkanth listened intently, his brows furrowed with cautious hope.

"Once this survey is complete," Mr. Bhujbal continued, "we plan to initiate rainwater harvesting training for all villagers. That will be crucial for your long-term survival, especially in a hilly region like this where groundwater recharge is a challenge. Until then, on MLA Sir's instructions, two water tankers will be sent daily to ensure no one sleeps thirsty."

Then, with a pause and a kind but firm look, he added,

"But we need your help. Ask everyone to use water wisely. Every drop saved today is a breath saved for tomorrow."

Nilkanth folded his hands with deep gratitude.

"Thank you, sir. We'll cooperate fully. This village has survived on faith and unity—and now, we will survive with your support too."

The village Sarpanch and other elders openly admired Nilkanth for stepping forward and respectfully probing the survey team. It was through his calm yet determined voice that the engineers had opened up, turning confusion into clarity. His gesture brought reassurance to the villagers—someone was asking the right questions on their behalf.

With renewed energy, the community waited patiently for the end of the survey. Within a week, the engineers and officials organized a training session on rainwater harvesting techniques. Under the shade of banyan trees and makeshift tents, the villagers listened carefully as experts explained how to trap and conserve rainwater through simple, cost-effective methods. They took notes, asked questions, and returned home with a hopeful heart, believing that the coming monsoon would not just bring rain—but freedom from thirst.

Soon after, the surveyors completed their ground assessment. They had used Remote Sensing technology and Satellite Imaging to scan the terrain. The results pointed out a handful of hidden groundwater reserves deep beneath the village, where faint traces of water remained. Some of these locations had once been shallow wells, long forgotten. The team marked the spots with red flags and chalk. The surveyors also motivated the villagers for afforestation, planting more trees in and around the village.

But there was a catch.

The water laid beneath thick layers of hard basalt rock, and accessing it, as per the engineers' conclusion, would be a herculean task—one that required heavy drilling machinery, permissions, and substantial funding and above all in a populated village such machineries could never be erected. The engineers, despite their efforts, admitted they could go no further. For the villagers, the hope flickered dim once again.

Yet for Nilkanth, even a dim spark was something sacred.

One of those water points—surprisingly—was just beside his own doorstep, where an old well had once quenched the thirst of his ancestors. It had dried up years ago and was now sealed with a flat stone lid, forgotten like a lost memory. That evening, Nilkanth sat near the old well, staring at the stone, his calloused fingers brushing away dry leaves as if seeking permission from the past.

"If water still lies beneath," he thought, "then maybe... just maybe... my home can bring life not just to my family, but to the entire village."

For an idol-maker, breaking through hardened rock seemed impossible.

But Nilkanth had spent his life shaping gods out of dust.

This time, he would try to shape hope.

After several weeks of persistent struggle and waiting, a wave of relief finally swept through the village. The long-promised pipeline from the Kajali River was connected, and for the first time in months, water flowed from communal taps. Children splashed their faces, women filled their copper pots with quiet gratitude, and elders offered prayers beside the gushing streams.

But the joy was measured.

The supply was limited, regulated by the government to conserve reserves for the approaching summer. Water flowed only twice a day, and each household had to gather at designated points, collecting their share with discipline and care. It was not abundance—but it was survival.

Nilkanth, ever practical and farsighted, knew this was not the end of their struggle—it was only a pause. Alongside the Sarpanch and village elders, he helped draw a detailed action plan to implement rainwater harvesting across the village. The goal was clear: before the next monsoon arrived, the village must be ready to capture every drop that touched its soil.

Soon, work began with tireless energy. Teams were formed. Pits were dug across fields, near community spaces, and alongside old dried wells. Canals were carved with careful slopes, angled to channel rainwater from rooftops and higher ground into collection pits and storage tanks. The village school became a hub of innovation. Nilkanth, along with his students, turned lessons into labour—teaching the science of harvesting through the act of digging, shaping, and building.

Their hands were muddy, their backs ached—but their spirits soared.

In the echoes of shovels and spades, a new kind of festival was being celebrated—not with lights and drums, but with hope, sweat, and the rhythm of self-reliance.

With the water crisis finally under control, Nilkanth felt a long-held burden ease from his chest. Without wasting time, he called Vinayak and asked him to come home—his summer vacation still had a few days left. Back at home, Savitri, Seema, and Ramesh were thrilled at the thought of seeing him after so long. The house had already begun to hum with quiet preparations: Savitri was planning his favorite meals, Seema was airing out his bedding, and Ramesh sat polishing his old radio, hoping to spend evenings with his grandson.

But then came a surprise none of them expected.

Vinayak hesitated.

He spoke softly over the phone, making excuses about study routines, and how it was more "convenient" to stay at Joshi Kaka's residence in Pune. Savitri, who knew her son's voice better than her own pulse, sensed something was off. This wasn't the same homesick boy who once cried on his hostel bed after a week away.

After the call, she sat down quietly, her eyes brimming with tears.

"Why doesn't he want to come home, Nilkanth? Has he changed so much?"

Her voice cracked under the weight of longing. "I miss him so much. Tell him he must come back. His vacation ends in just two weeks—I want him home, even if it's only for a few days."

Nilkanth sighed, gently putting his arm around her. But Savitri wasn't done. After a moment of silence, she looked at him and asked,

"Can you understand why Vinayak wants to stay back?"

Nilkanth shook his head slowly.

"I'm as surprised as you are. Maybe… maybe it's still the memory of the water crisis. Maybe he doesn't want to return to all that pain."

Savitri's eyes narrowed with quiet intuition.

"Your friend Shankar Joshi… he has a daughter, doesn't he? What's her name?"

Nilkanth thought for a second.

"Jayashree. She's about a year younger than Vinayak, I think."

That was enough.

Savitri's expression shifted—part knowing, part annoyed. She stared at the mobile phone lying on the table and sighed dramatically.

"So that's the story! A young boy, living under the same roof with a girl his age… and you didn't even think twice before sending him there? Nilkanth, what were you thinking?"

Nilkanth looked startled.

"Savitri, please. I never imagined anything like that. Vinayak's not that kind of boy. He's focused, grounded—"

Savitri interrupted with a raised eyebrow.

"Grounded or not, he's still human. And at that age, even the calmest boys can lose their footing. I'm not accusing him, but I know how young hearts work. If something goes wrong, we'll be blamed too. It's better he comes home."

Nilkanth, surrendering to his wife's concern, gave a sheepish smile.

"You may be right. I'll call Shankar Bhav now and ask him to send Vinayak tomorrow morning."

Savitri, still holding her mother's instinct close to her chest, nodded in quiet victory—her son was coming home.

Chapter 4

The Unexpected Days

The next morning, as the phone rang and Shankar Bhav informed Nilkanth that the bus from Pune had departed with Vinayak aboard, Savitri let out a long, deep breath—a blend of peace, relief, and motherly anticipation. She immediately began preparing Vinayak's favorite dishes, her bangles clinking softly as she moved around the kitchen.

Nilkanth, though happy, felt a quiet unease stirring inside him. Savitri's words from the night before had shown a few doubts in his heart—uncomfortable questions he hadn't asked himself as a father before.

Seated in the courtyard, Nilkanth shaped the clay with practiced hands, working on a new idol. But his fingers moved slower than usual. His thoughts wandered—could Vinayak truly have slipped into a romantic relationship? At this age? He couldn't help but question his own parenting. Had he given Vinayak too much freedom? Or had he, perhaps, been too consumed by responsibilities to truly talk about love and choices?

As he pressed the clay into the shape of an arm, he felt an urgency to speak—not to Vinayak, but to Savitri.

Carrying a lump of clay in one hand, he rushed inside. Savitri was by the stove, her dupatta tucked at the waist, frying pooris.

She turned around and yelped in irritation,

"Have you gone mad, Nilkanth? I'm cooking! Don't bring that sticky thing near the kitchen. Now, what is it?"

Nilkanth paused, sheepish, the clay slowly drying in his palm.

"Savitri," he said gently, "I don't know if we've become too judgmental about Vinayak. Maybe there's nothing going on. But even if there is... let's not jump to scolding or suspicion. Let's not make him feel guilty for something we've only assumed."

She looked at him, half-listening, half-annoyed, still holding the slotted spoon in her hand.

"You know how kids are at this age," he continued. "They believe they're right, no matter what we say. If we confront him with anger, he'll shut down. We should listen, probe gently—with care, not criticism. Let's be parents first."

Savitri's sternness softened.

She lowered the flame and turned toward him fully, her expression quiet.

"You always think I'm too harsh," she said with a sigh, but there was no real fire in her voice. "I know you care more deeply than I ever admit. And you're right. He must not make decisions in haste—especially when it comes to relationships.

But don't worry. I won't scold him. We'll both speak to him—with love."

Nilkanth smiled and placed the clay gently on the windowsill. In that moment, they weren't just a husband and wife—they were partners in the delicate art of parenting, trying to hold their son close without pulling too tight.

By the time the sun dipped behind the hills, casting a soft orange glow over the village, Vinayak finally arrived home. As he pushed open the familiar creaking gate and stepped inside, the smell of his mother's cooking mingled with the earthy scent of home—a scent no city could ever replicate.

Before he could even reach the veranda, Savitri rushed out of the main door, her eyes brimming with tears. She wrapped him in a tight embrace, burying her face into his shoulder.

"Missed you so much, beta," she whispered, her voice trembling. "You must be tired… come in."

Vinayak's face carried a strange mix of calm and unease. His smile was faint but genuine—the kind that blossoms when a long-held ache finds rest. Despite the weight in his eyes, he felt a quiet joy stirring inside him just being back. At the doorstep stood Seema and Ramesh, waiting like sentinels of love.

Vinayak immediately bent down to touch their feet.

Seema held his face between her palms, kissed his forehead, and said softly,

"My child, your absence… it was heavy. For a whole year, every corner of this house missed your voice."

Ramesh, always a man of fewer words, patted his grandson's back and added with a gentle smile,

"You must be tired. Go freshen up, and then join us for lunch. We've been waiting all day."

Vinayak nodded and stepped inside, his heart swelling quietly. This home, with its worn walls and warm hearts, still held a place for him—whether or not he was ready to explain the distance he had kept.

After dropping Vinayak at home from the bus stand, Nilkanth headed straight to the local market, picking out the freshest fish and vegetables. It had been a while since the house felt this alive, and he wanted to make the evening special. As he returned, climbing the familiar slope towards his home, he could already hear the echoes of laughter—Vinayak's voice mingled with Seema's teasing and Ramesh's dry humor. The sound poured out of the house like a melody he hadn't heard in months.

A tired but happy smile stretched across Nilkanth's face. This is what he had longed for.

He walked into the courtyard, set down the grocery bags, and made his way to the kitchen. Savitri was at the stove, the air fragrant with spices and warmth. She turned and gave him a knowing smile.

"Oh, we were all waiting for you to return," she said, brushing a strand of hair from her face. "Get fresh—I'm serving dinner."

Nilkanth leaned against the doorframe and asked quietly, "So? Got any clues?"

Savitri paused for a second, and then shook her head gently.

"No... nothing yet. But let's wait. I can sense something shifting in him—he laughs, then suddenly drifts off. His eyes don't lie."

Nilkanth sighed, placing a reassuring hand on her shoulder as he passed.

"Hmm... you might be right. But I doubt he'll confess. You know how children are at this age—full of feelings, but afraid to speak."

Savitri smiled faintly, her hands busy, her heart quietly watching.

"Then let's not force it. Let's give him what he came for—home. Maybe that'll make him speak without us asking."

Nilkanth nodded, carrying her words with him like an unsent letter. In the laughter echoing through the house, both parents were listening—not just with ears, but with hearts full of patient love.

At night after the dinner, Vinayak quietly stepped out of the house, saying something vague about taking a walk to clear his head. But Savitri knew better. There was a particular lightness in his footsteps, a quiet eagerness in the way he grabbed his phone, which gave her all the clues she needed.

She stepped out onto the small balcony, careful not to make a sound, and peeped down onto the dimly lit street. There he was—Vinayak, pacing slowly, phone held close, his face glowing not just from the screen but from something deeper.

And then it began.

The hushed tones, the sudden chuckles, that soft, teasing lilt in his voice... It wasn't just a call—it was someone special.

Savitri stood still, a strange mix of amusement and emotion swelling in her heart. She hadn't seen this boyish glow during dinner. This joy, this charm—it was love, unmistakably love.

Just then, she felt a faint breath on her shoulder. Startled, she turned—and smiled.

It was Nilkanth, silently standing beside her, watching his son with the same curiosity.

They said nothing.

Below them, Vinayak leaned against a tree, the faint orange light of the streetlamp catching his smile, his expressive eyes, and the way he kicked pebbles like a boy half his age. He was whispering, laughing softly—a language lover speaks when the world sleeps.

They stood watching him for a few minutes, until Savitri whispered,

"Now do you believe me?"

Nilkanth nodded slowly, a small smirk playing on his lips.

"He's my son. I really couldn't imagine."

After nearly an hour, Vinayak returned—his steps light but cautious. He opened the gate with the gentleness of a thief, closed the door behind him as quietly as possible, and tiptoed toward his room.

What he didn't know was—his parents, behind their closed eyes, were smiling. Pretending to be asleep, they held back their laughter, like old lovers who now shared a secret about a new one being born.

Even after the house had surrendered to silence, Savitri lay wide awake, her eyes fixed on the ceiling while the slow ticking of the wall clock filled the room. Yet, it wasn't the clock that kept her up—it was the soft hum of Vinayak's voice, drifting faintly from behind the closed door of his room.

The whispers, the stifled laughter, the drawn-out pauses between sentences—it was clear the conversation hadn't ended when he returned from his walk. It was still alive, thriving, unfolding with all the intensity of young love.

Savitri turned on her side, facing Nilkanth in the soft moonlight that filtered in through the window.

"I can still hear him talking," she whispered.

"This boy doesn't know when to stop. I will talk to him tomorrow—he must control himself. He's losing sense of time."

Nilkanth opened one eye, half-smiling, half-sighing.

"Let him have this night, Savitri. We can talk tomorrow. Love doesn't knock often… and when it does, it makes fools out of all of us."

Savitri huffed softly, but the corner of her mouth curled into a reluctant smile.

"Still, there must be some limits. He's not a child anymore, nor is he fully grown. We'll speak to him—not to scold, but to guide."

Nilkanth reached out and gently placed his hand over hers. "Exactly. Not to question, but to listen first."

Outside, the trees swayed softly in the seashore breeze of summer. Inside, two parents lay quietly—restless not with anger, but with care, caught between memories of their own past and the delicate beginning of their son's.

The morning sun filtered through the wooden windows, bathing the house in soft golden light. After breakfast, as Vinayak lingered near the kitchen sink rinsing his plate, Savitri wiped her hands and said casually,

"I'll need to unpack your luggage today. Give me all your unwashed clothes—I'll sort them for the laundry. Come, let's get it done."

Vinayak froze for a moment, his back stiffening. He turned around, trying to compose his face, but a flicker of panic flashed in his eyes.

"Uh… Aai, I'll do it myself," he said quickly, forcing a smile. "No need to trouble yourself. I'll put everything in the laundry bag."

Savitri raised an eyebrow, her tone sharpening just enough to poke him.

"Oh really? So now there's something in there you don't want me to see?"

She folded her arms, her eyes narrowing—not out of anger, but with the unmistakable look of a mother who knew her child was hiding something.

"Don't forget, Vinayak," she continued, "I used to pack and unpack your schoolbag till your higher classes. I even found your hidden secrets ...... remember?"

Vinayak's ears turned red. "Aai! That was years ago."

"Exactly! Which means I have experience," she replied with a smirk.

Vinayak shook his head in defeat, muttering, "It's not like that... I've just... become used to doing things on my own."

But before she could say more, he darted toward his room, nearly tripping over his own feet. Inside, he flung open his suitcase, quickly pulling out a shirt, then his notebook, then a small envelope—something he held for an extra second before tucking it deep into the back of the drawer.

Back in the living room, Nilkanth sat cross-legged with his newspaper, pretending to read, but his ears were tuned to every word.

He glanced over the top of the paper at Savitri, who now stood with hands on her hips at the door of Vinayak's room, watching the frenzied unpacking with quiet amusement.

"So..." Nilkanth said, without looking up from his paper, "Found a secret treasure, did he?"

Savitri smirked. "Not yet. But there's definitely a hidden gem buried somewhere."

Nilkanth chuckled softly to himself. The drama had just begun.

After clearing the breakfast plates, Savitri glanced around the house with practiced eyes—checking corners, listening for footsteps, scanning for the presence of her ever-curious in-laws. Once she was sure the coast was clear, she turned to Nilkanth, lowering her voice.

"Where's Aai and Baba?"

Nilkanth, still lounging with his half-folded newspaper, gave her a knowing smile.

"It's Ekadashi, remember? They've gone to the temple... your runway is clear."

He winked playfully, then added with a grin,

"Proceed, Commandant."

Savitri rolled her eyes but couldn't hide her smirk. She took a deep breath, smoothed the edge of her saree, and marched straight into Vinayak's room, where he was still pretending to rearrange a mess that looked suspiciously like it was made in haste.

"I asked you to let me unpack!" she called out from the doorway, her voice playful yet edged with authority.

"Now tell me—what exactly are you hiding, dear son?"

Vinayak startled, fumbling with a stack of papers that were clearly unrelated to laundry. His face flushed, and his words stumbled out.

"N-nothing, Aai! Just… trying to gather some notes, I—I need to staple them."

Savitri let out a soft chuckle and stepped one foot inside, arms crossed.

"Staple the truth instead, Vinayak." She narrowed her eyes.

"Come on, just tell us—what is her name? Who is she?"

Vinayak froze.

There it was. The question he knew was coming, but still wasn't ready to answer. His eyes dropped to the floor, a sheepish smile slowly forming on his face.

From the hallway, Nilkanth called out, barely able to contain his amusement—

"Don't take too long, beta. Your Aai has a PhD in sniffing secrets!"

Savitri added softly now, walking closer, her voice tender but unwavering—

"We're not angry, Vinayak. We just want to know the person who's brought that sparkle back to your eyes."

Vinayak looked up, caught between embarrassment and the warmth of being truly seen.

"Her name is Jayashree," he said at last, voice quiet but clear.

"Shankar Kaka's daughter."

Savitri blinked once, then twice—pretending to be surprised, though her heart had already guessed.

"So I was right," she murmured, shooting a glance at Nilkanth who peeked around the doorframe with an expression that said I knew it too.

Vinayak sat silently on the edge of his bed, his shoulders slumped, his eyes fixed on the window as if the answers were hidden somewhere in the trees swaying outside. His back faced his parents, perhaps to shield his emotions, or maybe because he didn't yet have the courage to meet their eyes.

Savitri, standing near the door, exchanged a glance with Nilkanth and gestured quietly for him to go speak. Nilkanth nodded, folded his newspaper, and stepped into the room with the gentle weight of a father's concern.

He sat beside his son and put a hand around his shoulder, pulling him into a soft embrace.

"Beta," he began, his voice warm and low,
"We're not scolding you… and we're certainly not angry."
He paused, letting the moment breathe.
"At your age, these feelings are natural. It's not love that worries us—it's the way you've been lost in it."

Vinayak's head remained lowered, but he leaned ever so slightly into his father's touch.

"You're our only son," Nilkanth continued, "and we've raised you with values, not wealth. I'm not a rich man who can hand you a future on a silver plate. You'll have to build it yourself—with knowledge, with effort, with pride."

Vinayak nodded, slowly, his fingers tightening into fists on his lap.

Then, in a voice barely above a whisper, he spoke—

"But Baba… I love her. Truly. I'm not playing games. I'm not taking any chances with her."

From the other side of the bed, Savitri had been listening quietly, her eyes reading every tremor in her son's voice. Now, she finally spoke.

"And does she love you the same way, Vinayak?" she asked gently.

"Have you spoken about your life here—our family, our village, our struggles?"

"I believe she understands," he said, glancing at his mother briefly.

"She's not like others, Aai… she's simple, grounded."

Nilkanth gave a soft smile and nodded.

"Then take time to understand each other more. If you're serious, we'll talk to Shankar Bhav and Deepa Vahini. But you both need to grow, complete your studies, and begin your careers first. Build a life you can offer her—not just dreams."

Savitri's voice was firmer now, but still kind.

"You're only twenty, beta. You have so much ahead of you. Don't rush into anything. Love needs time to mature—just like people. Once you earn something, and stand on your own feet, we'll bless your decision and stand by you. And if Jayashree remains with you through this journey, we'll welcome her with open arms."

Nilkanth tapped Vinayak's back cheerfully, trying to lift the mood.

"So… enough of this sulking! Be normal, be free. Give yourself and your love some time. That's how you'll know it's real."

Vinayak finally looked up. A faint, grateful smile tugged at his lips.

In that moment, he wasn't just a son confessing his first love—he was a boy growing into a man, with his parents walking beside him.

Savitri smiled softly at Nilkanth, her heart a little lighter after their conversation with Vinayak. She touched his arm gently and said,

"I think he understood what we meant. At least, I hope so."

Nilkanth nodded silently, then stood up to leave the room—it was Sunday morning, his favorite time for gardening. As he stepped outside with his gloves and tools, Savitri followed him, still draped in her casual cotton saree, the scent of coconut oil lingering faintly in the morning air.

Standing beside him in the little courtyard where bougainvillea crept over the low fence, Savitri leaned on the garden post and asked quietly—

"Do you think the match will really work, Nilkanth? I mean… tell me more about Shankar Bhav's family. What kind of people are they?"

Nilkanth paused while adjusting a young sapling, then smiled and replied,

"Shankar Bhav was a year senior to me in school. His father worked in the district administration, very strict man, and his mother was a homemaker. You remember that blue house next to the GaonDevi temple, near Sanichari Bazaar?"

Savitri nodded quickly.

"Yes, yes—the one with the peepal tree in front?"

"Yes! That's the one," Nilkanth said.

"They lived there before his father got transferred to Pune right after Shankar finished his metric. He has three elder sisters, and he's the only son. After they moved, he didn't come back often, except occasionally—one of his maternal aunts is married here in our village, so he visited sometimes."

Savitri's curiosity flared.

"Do you know that aunt? Can we meet her once?"

Nilkanth chuckled, wiping his hands on a towel and turning to her.

"Savitri, hold on! Why are you getting so anxious?" He softened his tone, adding gently,

"Let Vinayak settle first. Let them both grow and be sure of each other. Then, if things still look strong—we'll go ahead with all the plans… including meeting Shankar Bhav's relatives."

Savitri exhaled slowly, her eagerness gently melting into patience.

"You're right," she murmured.

"But you know me—I just want everything to be perfect for our son."

Nilkanth reached over and patted her shoulder with a smile.

"And that's why you're the best mother he could have."

For Vinayak, the weight on his chest had eased since he shared his heart with his parents. The silent tension that once brewed beneath his hesitation now dissolved into comfort. His parents hadn't scolded, hadn't judged—instead, they had listened, truly listened. They had given him space, and in return, he had learned where to draw his own lines, to let love grow with responsibility.

Perhaps in these fifteen days of summer, he and Jayashree had found a silent agreement—they would not rush, they would walk together only when they both felt ready to shoulder the future.

On the morning of his return to college, the house bustled quietly with mixed emotions. As Vinayak zipped his bag, he walked into the kitchen where Savitri was drying steel tiffin boxes in the morning sun. He stood there for a few moments, then softly said—

"Aai... Jayashree hasn't told anything to her parents yet. She's scared. Do you think Baba can… you know, casually hint something to Shankar Kaka?"

Savitri looked up, the corners of her eyes wrinkling with affection.

She smiled gently and wiped her hands on her saree.

"You focus on your studies, beta. Leave the rest to us. Don't worry. If Bappa has decided to bring Jayashree into our lives, it will happen—no one can stop that. I'll think of something... maybe we can invite her family during Ganapati. You will have to come home then, no excuses."

Vinayak's eyes lit up, a sudden brightness of hope filling his face. Without another word, he hugged his Aai tightly, burying his smile into her shoulder like he used to as a little boy.

As he stepped out of his room, bag slung over his shoulder, he found the entire family waiting for him—his Aaji and Ajoba standing with folded hands and smiles, his father near the gate holding the helmet.

He bent to touch the feet of his grandparents, who blessed him with trembling palms and glistening eyes. Nilkanth handed him the helmet and placed a firm but loving hand on his shoulder.

"Go make us proud, Vinayak," he said.

And with that, Vinayak left—not just for college, but with a heart fuller than ever before.

As Ganeshotsav arrived, the entire Konkan region burst into celebration—vibrant colours, devotional music, and a sense of spiritual joy that could make even the most burdened hearts feel lighter. At the Jadhav household, preparations had begun weeks in advance. Nilkanth's skilled hands shaped the idol with unmatched devotion, while Savitri decorated the house with strings of marigold and fresh rangoli patterns.

This year, Nilkanth and Savitri had decided to invite the Joshi family from Pune to join their ten-day celebration.

Knowing that the Joshis hosted Ganpati only for three days, Nilkanth hoped that the extended stay at their home might allow Vinayak and Jayashree to share space in plain sight—with honesty, warmth, and familial grace.

Shankar Bhav agreed with delight. But it was his wife Deepa who carried unexpected coldness beneath her urbane charm. Savitri, ever the gracious host, welcomed her with warmth—preparing meals to her liking, offering her the best seat during the puja, and making sure Jayashree felt at home.

One afternoon, while preparing modaks together in the kitchen, Savitri delicately broached the topic of Vinayak and Jayashree.

"They are still young," she said softly, "but they understand each other. I believe there's something beautiful blossoming there."

Deepa paused, wiped her hands, and responded with an icy calmness that pierced through Savitri's hope.

"Jayashree is meant for more. She's ambitious. She has a bright future ahead. Your son is still in college, and honestly, I don't think a village boy—however well-mannered—can match what we've envisioned for our daughter."

The words stung. Not because Savitri was unaware of their rural limitations, but because they reduced everything—values, love, integrity—to a postal pin code. She didn't argue. She simply walked out to the courtyard, her silence heavier than any retort.

That evening, after the evening aarti, as the lamps glowed around Bappa's idol, Savitri quietly told Nilkanth about Deepa's harsh words.

He didn't respond immediately. He continued placing fresh hibiscus flowers around the idol, as if drawing calm from Bappa himself. Then he turned to Savitri and said gently but firmly:

"I will speak to Shankar Bhav. We don't need to justify our son's worth to anyone. He may still be a student, but he has character, clarity, and roots—qualities far rarer than degrees and city lights."

Savitri nodded. The disappointment lingered in her heart, but Nilkanth's quiet strength rekindled her faith. This was not just about two young hearts. It was about the dignity of believing in one's upbringing and values.

While the Ganesh Puja continued with devotional chants and incense swirling in the air, Deepa's eyes often wandered from the idol to the subtle exchanges between Jayashree and Vinayak—the way their glances met during the aarti, how Jayashree adjusted the garland Vinayak had made for her hair bun, or how their laughter merged softly as they helped in arranging the prasad.

Deepa wasn't blind. She was just resistant.

Later that evening, while Jayashree was folding the puja dupattas in the corner of the verandah, Deepa called her aside. Her voice was low, sharp, and lined with a discomfort she didn't bother to mask.

"Jayashree, I noticed what's going on. Do you seriously see yourself in this clumsy village? No air conditioning, no proper bathroom fittings, not even a decent car in the porch. Just clay, mud and cowsheds? Is this the life you want?"

Jayashree lowered her eyes. She had expected this, yet her mother's words still pierced her.

"Savitri was hinting at something this afternoon—talking about your supposed 'inclination' for Vinayak. I shut it down immediately. That woman is clever; she wants to trap you into this slow, stagnant life, a village without proper water resources. But you deserve better. You know that, right?"

Jayashree's eyes welled up. Her voice cracked, but her words were clear:

"Aai, I do love Vinayak. It's not about being trapped—it's about being with someone who makes me feel grounded and safe. I know this village is not what I'm used to... and I don't plan to shift here permanently. But whenever we visit, I'll adjust. It's his family. His roots."

She paused, wiping her cheek with the edge of her dupatta.

"After marriage, we can work and live in Pune or Mumbai. I want a future with him—but I also want your blessings. Please don't let where he lives blind you to who he is."

For the first time, Deepa saw her daughter not as a child, but as a young woman willing to step beyond comfort for love. The silence that followed wasn't agreement, but it wasn't rejection either. It was a pause of realization—one that signaled a crack in Deepa's wall of resistance.

Deepa was deeply offended by her daughter's mindset, yet she felt helpless—Jayashree's words carried a conviction that was hard to shake. Still, Deepa resolved to try once more, hoping for a change of heart.

The next day was Anant Chaturdashi—the auspicious culmination of the ten-day Ganeshotsav. The Joshi family was scheduled to leave for Pune the following morning. As part of the farewell rituals, Jayashree and Vinayak walked together toward the sea beach to immerse the idol of Lord Ganesha.

On the way, Jayashree softly told Vinayak that she had already spoken to her mother about the two of them. "Now," she added, "it's up to our parents to decide."

Vinayak remained uncertain about how her mother would react, but as he bid farewell to Ganapati, he silently prayed for a special blessing—for the strength and grace to nurture their love.

The air was still damp with devotion as the last of the Ganesh immersion procession faded into the twilight. The rhythmic beats of the dhol had subsided into silence, leaving only the sound of waves brushing against the shore. Nilkanth and Shankar sat quietly on a stone bench under the banyan tree, where they had often shared stories of youth, dreams, and fatherhood.

Nilkanth broke the silence.

"Shankar Bhav… I wanted to share something with you. It's about Vinayak and Jayashree."

Shankar looked at him with a curious smile.

"Hmm? What about them?"

Nilkanth hesitated for a moment, his voice heavy with emotion.

"They're in love."

Shankar chuckled softly, more in recognition than in surprise.

"So… it's finally spoken out loud. You know, I always had a faint inkling. Vinayak stayed with us like he was our own son. Quiet, responsible, and so respectful. Jayashree and he… they often exchanged glances, shared laughs during dinner, helped each other with things—but it was always within bounds. I never saw anything improper. But now that you say it, it all fits."

Nilkanth nodded.

"Savitri noticed it first—the way he had changed. Less talkative, often lost in thoughts. One night, she gently asked him, and he opened up. It was hard for him too, to admit… But we were glad he trusted us."

Shankar looked out into the open sky, his expression soft.

"He's a fine boy, Nilkanth. Truly. I've told Deepa many times—if there's anyone I could wish for as my daughter's partner, it would be him. Quiet strength, clear values, and an honest heart. That's what matters."

Shankar placed a hand over his friend's shoulder.

"Shankar Bhav, having your trust means a lot. We didn't want to rush. That's why we invited your family during Ganpati—not just for the celebration, but to observe… to understand Jayashree better. And let me say this—she's an embodiment of grace, intellect, and humility. A true Laxmi. You and Vahini have brought her up so beautifully."

Shankar smiled, his eyes misting.

"These children have chosen each other with their hearts—and with time, maturity will shape that choice. Let's not rush them. But I will speak to Deepa. She needs time to see what I already do."

Nilkanth added warmly,

"There's no greater blessing for us than seeing our children complete each other's worlds. And for us as fathers… this is perhaps the most sacred moment—to trust the hands in which we place our children's futures."

As the two friends sat in content silence, a soft breeze passed between them—carrying with it the quiet promise of a shared tomorrow, built on trust, patience, and the enduring hope that love, when true, always finds a home.

Meanwhile, as the soft post-festival calm returned to the household, Savitri gently sat with her in-laws—Seema and

Ramesh—in the verandah, where the aroma of sandalwood and dried mango leaves still lingered from Ganeshotsav.

She took a deep breath, then spoke carefully.

"Aai, Baba... there's something I've been meaning to tell you. Vinayak and Jayashree... they've grown close. It began while he stayed with Shankar Bhav during his college term. It's more than friendship now—it's love."

Seema's eyes widened with joy, her hands instinctively joining in a soft prayer.

"Ganpati Bappa! I knew it! That girl has such grace in her every gesture. The way she helped me in the kitchen during Ganpati, the gentleness with which she speaks—truly she is made for our Vinayak." She paused, then leaned forward and added with delight, "Do you remember this purse?" She reached behind and pulled out a small embroidered handbag. "Jayashree gifted it to me that day—just like a daughter would. I forgot to show you. Such thoughtful children they are. I bless them with all my heart."

Savitri smiled warmly, touched by Seema's words, but her expression soon dimmed slightly.

"Aai... there's something more. Jayashree's mother, Deepa Vahini, isn't fully in favour of this match. She wants a wealthier groom for her daughter—someone with a city life, without water scarcity, all comforts, a car... not a village boy. We should give them all some time. Let the children grow, and maybe, hearts too will change."

Seema went silent for a moment, exhaling slowly. The gentle creases on her face deepened with thought. Then, with a quiet firmness, she stood up and walked to the old wooden trunk by the corner of the room. She opened it and retrieved a small velvet box wrapped in silk.

"Savitri," she said, holding out the box with reverence, "this gold bracelet belonged to my mother-in-law. I've kept it aside all these years—for the day my granddaughter-in-law enters this house. I don't care about riches or pride. If Vinayak sees a daughter in Jayashree, then I see one too. And when the time is right, this bracelet will rest on her wrist. You cannot resist me on this."

Savitri looked at her mother-in-law, moved beyond words. The love that came from acceptance—not wealth—was far more precious than gold.

Ramesh, who had been quietly listening, smiled gently and added, "Let destiny do its work. If Jayashree is meant to be here, no force can stop it. And if her love is true, even Deepa will see it one day."

Early morning sunlight filtered softly through the mango trees as the Joshi family prepared to leave for Pune. A quiet hush lay over the house, thick with unsaid emotions.

As part of the age-old Konkan tradition, Savitri stepped forward carrying a beautifully draped silk sari. Upon it, she placed the Shriphal (sacred coconut), green glass bangles, and gently marked Deepa's forehead with a touch of turmeric and vermilion—a gesture meant to bless and honour the elder woman of a departing family.

Then, Savitri, with folded hands and genuine humility, bent to touch Deepa's feet, seeking her blessings. Deepa, surprised by the warmth and reverence, blessed her with a smile and gently placed her palm on Savitri's head.

Seema followed, carrying a shimmering green and gold sari. She walked straight to Jayashree, placing the sari carefully in her arms. Her eyes brimmed with tears as she held the girl's face:

"Stay blessed, my child. May your steps bring peace and light wherever you go."

Savitri then came close, carrying a small red velvet box. She opened it to reveal a pair of delicate gold earrings. Placing them gently in Jayashree's hands, she embraced her and whispered with tearful affection:

"My Laxmi… my daughter… come soon. This home is waiting for the auspicious moment when your footsteps will cross this threshold forever."

Jayashree, overcome, lowered her gaze, nodded softly, and bowed to the elders in silence.

The Joshi family departed, the sound of their car receding down the narrow village road, leaving behind the scent of rituals, warmth, and longing.

As Savitri stood watching the empty gate, she turned to Vinayak, holding his hand firmly, and whispered:

"Beta… get settled soon. Don't keep your Laxmi waiting."

Vinayak opened his mouth to respond, but hesitation held him back. There was something unspoken in his eyes. He nodded faintly, the weight of his thoughts pressing against his silence.

That night, a strange stillness lingered in the house. The dinner plates were cleared, the kitchen cleaned, and the silence broken only by the flickering light of the television. Nilkanth and Savitri sat on the cane chairs, the warm scent of agarbatti floating in from the puja corner.

Vinayak, packed and ready to leave the next morning, sat cross-legged on the floor between them, his fingers nervously curling around the hem of his kurta.

After a few minutes of silence, he softly said,

"Aai… Baba… I need to talk to you about something Jayashree shared with me."

Savitri turned her head sharply, a faint crease of fear lining her forehead. She immediately muted the television and leaned forward.

"What is it, beta? Please don't hold anything back," she said, her voice trembling slightly.

Vinayak swallowed hard. He looked down, avoiding their eyes as his voice cracked under the weight of what he was about to say.

"Aai… after marriage… Jayashree and I won't be staying here in the village. We've discussed it. Her mother… she agreed to the marriage only on the condition that we live and work in either Pune or Mumbai. Jayashree… she's not ready to settle in the village as her parents feel that the water scarcity can arise any time. She says she'll try to adjust during visits… but not permanently…"

He trailed off, unable to speak further. The words hung in the air like a bitter smoke.

There was a long pause.

Nilkanth looked at Savitri. Savitri looked at Nilkanth. Their eyes mirrored the same quiet devastation—not anger, not shock—but the grief of something slipping away without warning.

Nilkanth's fingers gripped the armrest as he looked away towards the verandah, blinking rapidly. Savitri's lips quivered as she tried to speak, but no sound came.

She finally whispered, "So… this is the price we must pay… for love."

Vinayak, guilt pressing deep into his chest, reached for her hand,

"Aai… Baba… I didn't want to hide this. But we don't want to hurt you. We thought we could manage both. Please believe me… I love you both too much to ever forget my roots."

Nilkanth stood up slowly, walked toward the half-made idol in the verandah, and placed his palm gently on its clay shoulder. Without turning, he said in a heavy voice,

"This house... this village... this soil gave me everything I have, including you. I never thought I would have to watch my own son become a guest here."

Savitri, wiping the tear that escaped her eye, stood and walked over to Vinayak. She placed her hand on his head and said, "If it is love... we will never stop you. But you must promise us one thing—never forget the door of this house, and never let it remain shut for too long."

Vinayak looked up, his face drenched in guilt and love, and said,

"Never, Aai. Never, Baba. I promise."

The next morning dawned heavy with quiet emotions. The birds chirped as usual, the village stirred slowly, and the scent of tulsi leaves from the morning puja wafted through the courtyard.

Vinayak stood at the doorstep, his bag slung over one shoulder, his eyes moist but composed. He turned to Nilkanth, who was standing with folded arms near the verandah pillar, trying his best not to let his feelings spill.

Vinayak said softly,

"Baba... Shankar Kaka actually wanted Jayashree to stay here with us after our marriage."

He paused. "But both her parents... especially Deepa Aunty... they're still hesitant. Their biggest concern is the water scarcity. They feel... life here would be difficult for her."

Nilkanth sighed deeply, his eyes scanning the far-off hills beyond the mango trees. The morning sun caught the edge of the dried well outside their house—a silent witness to years of struggle and hope.

Vinayak continued, stepping closer,

"Maybe... if the water issue is resolved permanently, it'll help bridge that gap. Baba, I want her to feel this place is her home too."

Nilkanth nodded slowly, placing his hand gently on Vinayak's shoulder.

"You are right, beta. Water... it's not just about survival anymore. It's the thread that must stitch our family back together."

Just then, Savitri came out holding a small tiffin and a bottle of water. Her eyes met Vinayak's with quiet pride and aching affection.

"Here, something for your journey. And Vinayak..." she touched his cheek gently, "remember what Bappa gives us is always enough—but we must keep trying till He smiles again."

Vinayak touched the feet of Seema and Ramesh, who sat on the porch, their eyes glistening.

Ramesh cleared his throat, "Study well, and come back stronger."

Seema added, "And next time... bring Jayashree too. Even if just for a day."

With a deep bow and one last look at his home, Vinayak turned and walked down the familiar path to the bus stand, the morning sun lighting his way, while behind him, his family watched—holding hope like a prayer between clenched hands.

Chapter 5

The Phantasm of Hope

The days turned into months. The rainwater harvesting efforts showed modest results—a few water tube wells had begun to yield again, offering the village a flicker of relief. Yet for Nilkanth, a heavier burden had taken root—a gnawing fear that grew with every sunrise.

It was no longer just about water.

How could he embrace his son's future in this village now?

How would Vinayak find a respectable teaching job here, especially in a reputed Convent or English-medium school?

Would this land, with its warm soil and golden silence, ever be enough for his son's ambitions—or for the expectations of the girl he loved?

What had once been a family matter had now grown into a matter of pride. The words of the Joshi family lingered like an invisible wall between two homes, two worlds. They had planted doubt—a silent insult hidden in concern—and now that insult festered inside Nilkanth like an old wound.

Each day, as the birds chirped from the mango branches, as the Arabian Sea whispered on the distant shore, as children giggled and chased marbles under the banyan tree, as the house kitten darted out of the kitchen with a stolen crust of roti—in every small joy of the village, Nilkanth felt a pang.

"Will Vinayak miss all of this forever?" he wondered.

Will he be swallowed by the smog and clamor of the city?

Would he learn to love that life and forget this one—this sacred, imperfect life built with clay and calloused hands?

The thought shook Nilkanth deeply. He had lost many things to time, to drought, to silence. He could not lose his son—not to the city. Not to distance. Not to despair.

Most nights, Nilkanth found himself waking up in the middle of the night—restless, anxious, consumed by a silence too loud to ignore. He would sit on the edge of the bed, staring at the dim outlines of the idols in the courtyard, his mind pacing like a caged animal.

Savitri noticed the toll it was taking on him. His eyes, once steady with devotion, now seemed burdened with a silent storm. She grew increasingly worried—not just for his mind, but for his body too. The strain was showing.

At the same time, his parents' health had begun to deteriorate. Seema's blood pressure would spike without warning, and Ramesh's fading eyesight often left him groping for familiar things in their own home. The age that once only whispered now spoke loudly through every breath and falter.

One quiet afternoon, while sitting together on the veranda, Ramesh and Seema called Nilkanth and Savitri close. Ramesh held Nilkanth's hand and said, his voice quivering like an old stringed instrument:

"Beta, please arrange Vinayak's marriage soon. Our bodies are weakening... we may not be around for too long."

Seema added softly, almost like a prayer:

"We want to see our grandson take the next step before our eyes close. It would complete our journey."

Those words struck Nilkanth like a bell in a silent temple—clear, urgent, and echoing long after they were spoken.

Those words fell upon Nilkanth like an avalanche—not just a plea from aging parents, but a haunting echo of fear. It trembled him inside out, shaking loose the memories he had buried beneath routine and restraint.

He suddenly remembered Kartik, his childhood friend and living-next-door neighbor. Kartik, once surrounded by the laughter of children, now spent his days in silence with his sick wife. His two sons and daughter, all working in Mumbai, had abandoned him. They rarely called, never visited. Kartik often sat on the temple steps with misty eyes, yearning just to play with his grandchildren—a man breathing, but hollow.

Nilkanth felt that same fear rising in his chest—the fear of losing his son to the city, of watching his family splinter into distant voices and occasional visits. A life of unending solitude, where even love becomes memory and the house turns from home to echo.

His eyes filled uncontrollably. Turning to Seema and Ramesh, he said in a choked voice, barely able to contain the storm inside him:

"Yes, Aai… Baba… I will talk to Vinayak very soon."

Seema noticed the quiver in his tone, the wet shimmer in his eyes. Concerned, she asked gently:

"What made you cry, Beta? Is there resistance from the Joshi family? Or something else? Please tell me. I hope I haven't hurt you."

Nilkanth quickly brushed his tears with his fingers, attempting a smile that half-succeeded.

"Arey Aai! These tears... they came from happiness. Just the thought that our Vinayak has grown so much—that he is ready for marriage—made them burst out."

Seema, Ramesh, and Nilkanth all smiled together. But beneath that smile was a silent pact—an unspoken agreement to carry the weight of worry beneath blankets of joy.

Savitri, who was busy stitching some dresses near the window, suddenly received a call from Vinayak. She picked it up casually, but within seconds, something he said made her leap out of her chair. Her face lit up like the first morning sun after a long storm.

She exclaimed into the phone, "I'm so happy, Beta! Wait—don't go anywhere. Let me tell your father too!"

Without even disconnecting the call, she rushed to the verandah where Nilkanth was sitting with his parents. "Nilkanth!" she called out breathlessly, "Vinayak got a job as a Mathematics teacher at a school!"

Nilkanth turned toward her. A flicker of joy passed over the face of Nilkanth and his parents. But it was quickly followed by a subtle cloud of worry within Nilkanth. The word "job" now meant distance. He hesitated a moment, then took the phone from her with a smile that tried to hide his anxious thoughts.

"Congratulations, Beta! That's wonderful news. So—where is it? Is it a private school or government?"

From the other end, Vinayak's voice came clear and confident:

"Baba, I appeared for the Government Teacher Recruitment Exams, and I got selected! Because I belong to Ratnagiri district, they've offered me a post at a government school here—in Ratnagiri! It comes with good salary too. I think I can stay close to you all."

Nilkanth froze. For a moment, the world around him blurred. He couldn't believe what he had just heard. His hands trembled, but his heart danced. Tears of joy welled up silently and traced down his cheeks. A storm of relief burst through his chest as he stood up in joy.

"That's... That's amazing, Beta! Don't worry about anything—I'll take care of all the arrangements here. You come and join soon!"

Vinayak replied with certainty, "Yes, Baba! I'll be there this Sunday."

Vinayak's return was no less than a festival for the entire family. Joy wrapped every corner of the house—his grandparents beamed with pride, Savitri couldn't stop smiling, and Nilkanth seemed to walk lighter, as if a burden had lifted from his heart.

Soon, Vinayak's professional journey began. Each day, he traveled nearly an hour to reach his government school. Slowly, a bond grew between him and his students. He was no longer just Vinayak—the son of an idol maker—but a committed teacher who had inherited not just his father's artistic precision, but also his devotion and quiet sense of purpose.

Months passed. Vinayak threw himself into his work, shaping young minds with care and patience. His love life took a quiet pause, tucked away respectfully behind lesson plans and chalk dust. But Jayashree grew restless. One evening, over a phone call, she confessed, "Vinayak, my mother has started looking for a match within her family. I keep avoiding it, but I don't know how long I can."

Vinayak fell silent. Torn between the calling of his career and the tug of his heart, he sat quietly under the night sky, listening to the distant hum of crickets. He had always imagined love and responsibility walking hand in hand—but now, they stood like diverging roads.

A dilemma weighed heavily on his shoulders: Should he take the next step with Jayashree and risk shaking the fragile balance of his new career? Or should he wait, and perhaps lose the only girl he had ever loved?

One evening, Vinayak called Jayashree. As her voice came through the speaker, warm and familiar, he hesitated for a moment before speaking.

"Jayashree," he began, "if we are going to get married, I need to ask you something important... Would you be willing to live here with me and my family in the village? Since I've started working here, this is where our life would begin."

There was a pause on the other end, a brief silence that felt unusually heavy. Then Jayashree sighed and replied softly,

"Vinayak, you know how Aai feels about the village. She's always dreamt of something different for me—comforts, a city life, everything she never had. Convincing her won't be easy."

She paused again, then continued, her voice steadier,

"But I'm not saying no. I just want to work too. I've done my graduation in Computers—you know I'm good with both software and hardware. If I can get a job nearby, something that aligns with my education, I'll have a strong reason to convince her. It will show that I'm not giving up everything I've worked for."

Vinayak listened carefully, understanding the weight behind her words.

"That's completely fair," he said after a moment. "I'll start looking around here—maybe there's a way you can freelance or take on something small initially. But you may need to be here for that to work."

There was a smile in her voice when she replied,

"If it's with you, Vinayak, I'm ready to try. Just be patient with me—and with them."

Vinayak smiled too, though she couldn't see it.

"Always," he whispered.

It wasn't a perfect solution, but it was a shared hope—and that was enough for now.

Once again, Vinayak and Jayashree decided to speak to their parents and elders about their wish to marry—and this time, the discussions bore more hopeful results. Most family members began to lean positively toward the union, except for one persistent resistance: Deepa, Jayashree's mother. Deepa simply could not accept the idea of her daughter settling in a village, especially one still grappling with water scarcity and lacking the comforts of urban life. Practical, money-minded, and ego-driven, Deepa often called Jayashree an emotional fool for considering such a compromise.

Several heated arguments followed—between Deepa and Shankar, and between mother and daughter—until Deepa finally relented, but with a stern condition. She told Vinayak clearly:

"If my daughter ever finds it difficult to adjust to village life, you must agree—without resistance—to move to Pune. That is non-negotiable."

This clause, though accepted for the sake of peace, became a point of quiet concern for Savitri and Nilkanth. For them, Deepa represented not just a future in-law but a potential challenge to the health and harmony of their family's future. Savitri, rose on the belief that a married woman must treat her husband's family as her own and strive to nurture unity above all, found it hard to ignore the looming presence of Deepa's influence.

Jayashree, for her part, held a similar philosophy in her heart. Yet, Deepa's emotional hold over her—rooted in years of a close and dominant upbringing—was something she could neither deny nor easily break away from.

After navigating every bump and bend along the way, the long-awaited wedding finally took place in the crisp winter days of the following year. The two families came together, united by understanding and affection, and Vinayak and Jayashree were joined in the sacred bond of marriage. The celebration was nothing short of grand—gaga with joy—held at the heart of the village with over a hundred guests in attendance.

Nilkanth, ever the devoted artist, poured his soul into designing the décor and the wedding pandal at the community hall. Draped in flowers and handmade embellishments, the space bore his signature touch—graceful, earthy, and filled with devotion.

Jayashree's arrival into the Jadhav household marked more than a wedding—it was a quiet revolution. Her homecoming brought a new rhythm, a fresh fragrance, and a silent transformation that neither Seema, Ramesh, nor even Savitri and Nilkanth could have fully anticipated.

A new home, a new lifestyle, and a set of unfamiliar challenges—everything about village life was a significant shift for Jayashree. Yet, amidst this change, she felt blessed. Vinayak proved to be a loving and attentive husband, always by her side, gently easing her into the rhythm of her new world.

However, for Vinayak, his responsibilities were layered—his love and care for Jayashree ran deep, but so did his unwavering devotion to his parents and grandparents. He believed in balancing both, which sometimes made Jayashree feel caught in between.

Adding to the quiet strain, Deepa, her mother, often tried to plant doubts in her mind. She would be little Vinayak's humble life and question his priorities, warning that his excessive obedience toward his parents might someday create cracks in their marriage. Jayashree, though torn, held onto her instincts and love—but Deepa's words lingered like a shadow.

Although Deepa often voiced her disapproval, Jayashree never truly took her mother's words to heart. The depth of love, trust, and respect she received from Vinayak left no space for doubts—only gratitude. Her bond with Vinayak grew stronger with time, and the warmth she received from Savitri and Ajji (grandmother) made the village feel more like home with each passing day.

As days turned into months and then a year, Jayashree gradually carved a space for herself in the village. She began taking evening tutorial classes for local children, earning a modest but sufficient income. With that, she managed her personal needs and even lovingly bought small gifts for Savitri and Ajji—like sarees, cosmetics, and other thoughtful tokens of affection. In this simple, grounded life, Jayashree found quiet joy and a sense of belonging.

What began to worry Jayashree more than anything else was Ajji's declining health. The bond between the granddaughter-in-law and grandmother grew so deep that Seema seemed more emotionally dependent on her than ever before. At times, Jayashree would sit beside Ajji, helping her tie her hair, or they would watch web series and old films together on a smartphone, giggling like schoolgirls. Sometimes, Jayashree would even learn age-old recipes from her, their laughter echoing through the kitchen.

Savitri, though deeply affectionate towards her daughter-in-law, couldn't help teasing her now and then. "You're lucky, Bahu," she'd say with mock envy. "My Saasu Ma never pampered me the way she does you!"

Seema would shoot back with a playful grin, "Well, did you ever share your stolen laddus with me the way Jayashree does?"

That would send her into a loud cackle, her half-broken teeth gleaming as she smirked at Jayashree. Savitri would dramatically widen her eyes and shout, "Ah-ha! So that's why your sugar levels are climbing! I must tell your son, Aai!"

At once, Seema's expression would shift to playful fear as she pleaded, "Only once! That too during Ganapati! And I forced her to give it to me. Don't be angry, my dear!"

And just like that, the three women would dissolve into laughter, the house brimming with the joy of shared jokes and quiet love. That particular Sunday noon, just before Diwali, was especially merry as they sat together making festive snacks, their hearts full and their hands busy.

That Diwali was perhaps the last one when the Jadhav home glowed with lights in every corner—yet a shadow lingered in one corner of Nilkanth's heart. The diyas burned bright, the walls shimmered with rangoli and floral torans, but inside, Nilkanth remained preoccupied with the silently dropping water levels in the wells. Every villager had done their part with water harvesting, yet the results were slowly declining.

He hadn't shared his worries with anyone, but Savitri, ever tuned to her husband's moods, sensed the cloud in his silence, the weight in his shoulders. One evening, as they sat on the swing in the courtyard, she gently broke the silence.

"Don't worry," she said softly. "We'll manage again, as we always have. If needed, we'll take stricter steps at home. And... may be send Jayashree to her parents for a while."

Nilkanth looked at her, surprised. "Why send her away?"

Savitri smiled knowingly, her eyes sparkling like the diyas on the windowsill. "I have a feeling... a good news may be on the way."

Nilkanth's face lit up like the first sunlight breaking through storm clouds. "You mean... I'll become an Ajoba?"

Savitri quickly placed a finger on her lips. "Ssshhh! It's just a guess. But I've noticed—her food habits are changing, she tires more easily... I think I should take her to Dr. Leena. Just like Aai did with me."

She turned her gaze toward Seema, who sat at a distance on the sofa, humming softly while shaping warm laddus on a steel plate in her lap. The lamp beside her flickered gently, catching the glint of her smile, as if even she could feel something auspicious in the air.

The Diwali eve sparkled brighter than usual—Vinayak had brought home colorful lights and a bundle of firecrackers, spreading cheer across the Jadhav household. The front gate was lit with oil lamps, laughter echoed in the crisp evening air, and the scent of sweets wafted from the kitchen.

Vinayak was outside on the road, lighting a series of sparklers, while the rest of the family stood nearby enjoying the spectacle. Suddenly, without warning, Jayashree—standing beside Savitri—swayed and slumped onto her shoulder.

Startled, Savitri gasped, "Oh! Jayashree, what happened? Are you okay?"

Vinayak spun around, panic flashing in his eyes. "Jaya? What's wrong? Aai, what happened to her?"

Rushing over, he helped Savitri support Jayashree into the verandah. Savitri held her in her lap and said, "Vinayak, get some water—quickly. Sprinkle it on her face."

Jayashree slowly opened her eyes, still disoriented. She sat up slowly on Savitri's lap and murmured, "Aai... I don't know what just happened. I felt dizzy... and everything went blank."

Vinayak crouched beside her, his voice trembling, "Are you feeling okay now? Did you feel any pain?"
Jayashree nodded slightly, still groggy. "Just... dizziness. I couldn't control myself."

Seema, watching with concern, said gently, "Vinayak, bring her some water with sugar and a little salt. Her pressure must've dropped—she's been fasting for the puja, hasn't she?"

Vinayak rushed inside and returned with the glass. "Why didn't you tell me you were fasting? I would've stopped you."

As Jayashree slowly sipped, Savitri sat beside her, trying to hide a knowing smile behind the edge of her sari.

Vinayak looked at her, puzzled. "Aai, you're smiling? Right now? We're all worried here!"

Savitri glanced at Nilkanth, then smirked. "Because I guessed right. But let's wait for Dr. Leena's confirmation tomorrow."

Seema chuckled heartily and clapped her hands. "Oh ho! Vinayak, get ready. Your new firecracker partner is on the way!"

Vinayak blinked, confused. "What do you mean?"

Jayashree blushed deeply and looked away, sitting on the steps shyly.

Seema rolled her eyes with a grin. "You idiot! You're going to be a Baba! Understood now?"

Vinayak's eyes widened in disbelief, then slowly filled with a mix of awe, wonder, and pure joy. He turned toward Jayashree, and their eyes met—a thousand unspoken emotions passed between them under the Diwali stars.

The next morning, Jayashree and Vinayak visited Dr. Leena for a check-up. After a short examination and some tests, the doctor looked up with a gentle smile.

"Congratulations," she said warmly. "You're going to be parents. Jayashree, everything looks fine, but you must take good care of yourself in the coming months."

Jayashree beamed and teased softly, "Doctor, my husband is too caring. I don't think I can escape his care even if I try."

Dr. Leena chuckled. "That's how it should be. If all goes well, by the next rainy season, your home will be blessed with the cry of a twinkling little star."

The ride back home was filled with happiness—Jayashree couldn't stop smiling, and Vinayak held her hand tightly, his mind already dreaming of the future.

Back at home, the news burst into the household like a firecracker—Seema clapped in delight, Ramesh said a silent prayer of gratitude, and Savitri hugged Jayashree tightly with tear-filled eyes. The family was radiant with joy.

Except for Nilkanth.

He smiled, yes, and even hugged his son quietly. But deep inside, the shadow of worry lengthened. His heart once filled with dreams of clay and devotion, now pulsed with dread. The joy of a grandchild was tinged with the fear of whether this village—still battling water scarcity—could support a growing family.

As others celebrated, Nilkanth stood by the window, watching the well in the courtyard. The water had already begun to recede. The summer was near.

And the fear of losing everything he had kept so close—his son, his new daughter-in-law, the coming child—to the city's call for comfort and convenience began to gnaw at him more than ever before.

The joy of Jayashree's pregnancy continued to blossom through the spring, brightening the home all the way into Shimgotsav. Holi brought laughter, music, and vibrant colours into every corner of the Jadhav household. Jayashree, enveloped in the warmth of family and festivities, slowly began to let go of her memories of Pune. The love she received here—in this modest Konkan village—had begun to outweigh everything she had left behind.

But the morning after Shimgotsav, the air changed.

Alarming news spread like wildfire across the village: a deadly new virus—Corona—had begun to surge across the state. Rumours of lockdowns, hospital overloads, and containment zones created unease and fear.

Nilkanth came rushing into the house, his face tense. He found Vinayak in the courtyard and said firmly, "Beta, I don't think it's safe for Jayashree to stay here anymore. She's pregnant, and this virus is unpredictable. Before any lockdown is announced, you must take her to Pune. The medical facilities are better there. She'll be safer."

Vinayak was reluctant at first, but after speaking with the Principal of his school and some colleagues, he realized they all agreed. It was a practical decision—but not an easy one.

When Vinayak broke the news to Jayashree, her face fell. Her voice trembled as she asked, "You really want me to leave now, just when everything has started to feel like home?"

Vinayak gently held her hands. "No, Jaya. I don't want you to go. But I need you to be safe. We'll all be anxious here, knowing the situation could get worse quickly."

Jayashree wiped her eyes. "I've started loving this home more than anything. It hurts more than I imagined."

Savitri and Seema tried to stay strong, but as the bags were packed, tears refused to hold back. Seema hugged Jayashree tightly. "Beta, I will wait every day for your return. Take care of our grandchild."

Savitri added, stroking Jayashree's hair, "You're not going away—you're going to protect our blessing. That's what a mother does."

Jayashree nodded silently, resting her head on Savitri's shoulder. The fear of the pandemic loomed outside, but within those walls, it was love that made the parting most difficult.

Vinayak rushed to Pune and left Jayashree safely at her parents' home. The journey back felt like walking away from a part of himself, but he knew he had made the right choice. Meanwhile, Jayashree, despite being back in the house where she grew up, felt an unfamiliar and unexplainable solitude. It wasn't the walls of the house that made her feel alone—it was the absence of him, and the quiet rhythm of a village life she had come to embrace.

Days turned into weeks, and Jayashree found herself dwelling in a world shaped by memories—of Nilkanth's silent warmth, Savitri's playful scolding, and Seema's gentle laughter. She missed them deeply—not as in-laws, but as her own. To her, Savitri and Seema were like two beloved elder sisters, her guides, her support system.

Nearly every morning and evening, she would do video calls with Savitri and Seema, laughing through screens, sharing her meals, and sometimes quietly shedding tears together. At night, it was Vinayak who called. They'd speak for hours—sometimes teasing, sometimes dreaming, sometimes sitting quietly, saying nothing but listening to each other's breath.

Then came the long, grim months of lockdown. From 22nd March onward, the world seemed to stop moving. Shops shuttered, roads emptied, and sirens began to wail in the distance. The first wave of the pandemic struck like a storm, sweeping away normalcy. Both the Jadhav and Joshi families lost some close friends and distant relatives in that heart-wrenching summer. Grief, though unspoken, lingered like dust in the air.

In June, as the first rains returned to Konkan and the monsoon touched the soil, Jayashree stepped into her ninth month of pregnancy. The weight of life within her and the worry around her pressed down heavily. That was when Vinayak, unable to stay away, came back to Pune. As online classes started Vinayak worked from home and took utmost care of Jayashree.

Jayashree's parents had made all arrangements at a reputable hospital. Though masked and cautious, Vinayak returned as her pillar—ready to stand by her, no matter the risks. This time, it wasn't just about bringing her to safety—it was about being present when their child would arrive.

All of Jayashree's checkups had gone perfectly, and the doctors had reassured the family that both mother and child were healthy. On the morning of June 14, a sharp wave of pain struck Jayashree. Without wasting a moment, she was rushed to the hospital. The delivery was smooth—no complications, no surgical procedures—and soon after, Jayashree and Vinayak were blessed with a baby boy.

As the news reached the Jadhav household, the entire family erupted in joy. Seema's hands trembled as she folded them in prayer. Ramesh kept repeating Vinayak's childhood stories, tears welling up in his eyes. Savitri lit an oil lamp in front of the Ganpati idol, her smile unable to contain the whirlwind of emotions. For them, it was not just the birth of a child—it was the birth of new hope.

But amid the celebrations, Nilkanth sat silent, his joy muffled by an unshakable worry.

The water scarcity in the village had worsened again. The wells were drying up faster than expected. Though the pipelines still ran, their timing was erratic, and water levels were meager. The thought pierced him: How can I welcome my grandson into a home where we cannot even guarantee clean drinking water?

Earlier that week, Shankar had quietly shared the same concern during a phone call:

"Vinayak might have to think seriously now, Nilkanth. A baby changes everything—especially when survival becomes a matter of daily planning."

As the house rejoiced around him, Nilkanth's heart grew heavier. He slipped quietly into the puja room, folded his hands, and bowed before Siddhi Vinayak.

"Give me strength, Bappa," he whispered, "Don't let this family break apart. Help me protect them."

The next morning, unable to resist the pull of their grandchild's arrival, Nilkanth, Savitri, Seema, and Ramesh hired a cab and left for Pune. The four of them, brimming with anticipation, sat huddled together, rehearsing lullabies, jokes, and stories—eager to hold the baby who had already become the light of their lives.

But in a quiet corner of the cab, Nilkanth stared out at the highway, his eyes tracing the clouds. A grandfather now—but still a man burdened with fears only the rain could wash away.

As the cab speed past the winding roads of Konkan, laughter and excitement bubbled inside—until Seema suddenly furrowed her brow and snapped,

"Savitri! I'm sure you forgot the dress bag—and the box with the jewellery! How could you be so careless?"

Savitri, seated beside her, rolled her eyes and sighed loudly.

"Aai, for heaven's sake! I double-checked everything last night. Why don't you trust me?"

But Seema wasn't ready to back down.

"Stop the cab, Nilkanth! Just stop and check. I don't want to reach Pune and find we've forgotten the baby's gifts. This isn't a wedding where we can borrow things last minute!"

Nilkanth raised his hands helplessly and called out to the driver to pull over.

"Bappa re! This is what happens when excitement turns into panic," he mumbled under his breath.

Outside, on the roadside, Savitri yanked open the boot of the cab and pointed at the carefully packed bundles.

"Here! This is the bag of gifts, the gold bangles, the saree for Deepa, toys for the baby, ladoos for Shankar Bhav… Want me to unwrap and show each one?"

She glared at Seema, half-laughing and half-annoyed.

"Aai, I swear—you've gone completely mad with joy. If this is how you behave before seeing your great-grandson, I wonder what you'll do when you actually hold him!"

Seema pressed her lips together, trying to suppress a sheepish smile. Her eyes twinkled as she made a few exaggerated, teasing faces at Savitri like a child being scolded.

Ramesh, who had been quietly chuckling in the front seat, finally spoke up.

"Enough of your mother-daughter drama. Everyone, back in! The baby's waiting, and so are our blessings."

The cab resumed its journey as the sun raised higher, golden light painting the road ahead. Despite the squabbles and teasing, the love that bound them was unmistakable—full of warmth, tradition, and the kind of affection that only a family can carry.

Chapter 6

The Unendurable Days

The harsh summer sun peeked through the lazy, half-spread clouds, casting a shimmering glare on the quiet lanes of Pune. The humid air clung to their clothes, adding to the stickiness of anticipation and restlessness. After hours on the road and a handful of squabbles, the cab finally rolled to a gentle stop in front of the Joshi residence.

Before the engine could even fall silent, Nilkanth stepped out and rushed toward the entrance, his heart pacing faster than his feet. The house already echoed with the high-pitched cry of a newborn—raw, rhythmic, and alive. That cry pierced the heavy afternoon air and sent a thrill racing through Seema and Savitri.

The two women locked eyes, a current of joy passing between them. Their hands instinctively clutched one another's arms as if to hold steady the wave of emotion that surged up.

Nilkanth rang the doorbell with impatient fingers.

Within seconds, the door creaked open.

Vinayak stood there with a soft, exhausted smile, his eyes puffy from sleepless nights but sparkling with pride. Without a word, he stepped forward and bowed down, touching the feet of his parents and grandparents. As he straightened up, Savitri cupped his cheeks and whispered,

"You've become a 'Baba' now, yet you still look like my little boy."

Seema, teary-eyed, stepped forward, trembling slightly, and asked in a breathless voice,

"Where is he? Where's our little prince?"

Vinayak chuckled, stepping aside to reveal the living room bathed in soft daylight. On the far side, cradled in a swing made of muslin and gently swaying, was the newest member of the Jadhav family—tiny, pink, and wrapped like a sacred offering in white cotton.

The women gasped. Savitri moved as if in a trance, and Seema followed, muttering prayers under her breath. Nilkanth stood still at the threshold, his eyes moist, absorbing the miracle before him.

This wasn't just a house visit—it was the arrival at a new chapter in their story.

As they stood gathered around the cradle, their eyes fixed on the sleeping baby swaddled in soft white cloth, silence took hold. The little one lay with his fists curled beside his cheeks, a faint smile playing on his lips—as if he were dreaming of the love that awaited him.

Seema whispered, her voice trembling with awe,

"He's so adorable… a little version of Jayashree. Our lucky charm has arrived."

Savitri, her hands folded in reverence, added softly,
"A blessing from Bappa himself."

Just then, Jayashree entered the room, supported by Deepa and Shankar. She looked pale but radiant, her face glowing with the warmth of new motherhood. Despite her exhaustion, her eyes lit up upon seeing the Jadhav family.

Both families exchanged warm greetings, words of congratulations overlapping with laughter. The joy in the room was palpable, like a long-awaited monsoon after months of drought.

Sweets were offered on silver trays, hands reached out in affection and gratitude, and the air filled with the delicate smell of ghee and cardamom.

Jayashree settled into the sofa, holding her waist with one hand as she sat down gently. Savitri, noticing her fatigue, quickly stepped forward with the carefully packed gifts—a small gold chain, baby clothes, a silver anklet, and a hand-knit wool cap. She placed them beside Jayashree with care, saying,
"These are not just gifts, but blessings wrapped in love. You've made our home complete, beti."

Jayashree's eyes welled up, but she smiled and held Savitri's hand with silent gratitude.

For the next two days, laughter echoed through the Joshi household—between shared meals, exchanged memories, and moments when each of them took turns gently rocking the baby's cradle. In those hours, the weight of fears, doubts, and unspoken anxieties melted away, leaving only joy.

It was a time none of them would forget—a brief island of peace before life would, once again, start asking questions of them.

As both families sat together, sharing tea and sweets in the warm afternoon light, the conversation naturally drifted to the painful memories of the lockdown. They spoke in hushed tones of friends lost, long months of separation, and the silent fear that had gripped every home. Shankar and Deepa offered repeated advice on taking precautions, especially now that a newborn had entered their lives.

Jayashree listened quietly, her gaze often falling on her sleeping child, while Savitri and Seema nodded in agreement. Amidst the warmth of shared concern and familial bonding, the conversation suddenly took a heavier turn—the most unwelcome topic surfaced: the water crisis in the village.

Nilkanth, with a calm but firm voice, spoke with honesty.

"We're still struggling," he said. "The wells are drying faster than they can recover, and while our rainwater harvesting efforts have helped, they aren't enough yet. The entire village is working together, but until a stable solution is in place, Jayashree must stay here. Let her and the baby is safe. Vinayak can visit on weekends—and anyway, most of the teaching has shifted online after the lockdown. This arrangement is best, for now."

Everyone fell silent for a moment, the weight of reality sinking in. Deepa gave a small nod, satisfied with Nilkanth's clarity. Vinayak looked at his father with a mix of admiration and concern, understanding the silent burden Nilkanth carried every day for the sake of their home.

But eventually, Deepa slipped back into her familiar pattern of obsessive concern for her daughter's wellbeing. Her tone turned sharp as she looked directly at Nilkanth and said,

"I still believe Vinayak should request a transfer to somewhere near Pune. Why must he live so far when he now has a family? I don't think the water crisis in your village will ever truly be solved. I tolerated it while Jayashree was the one suffering, but now… even this poor baby is expected to endure the same?"

Her words fell like a blade in the room—cutting through the fragile warmth that had held both families together over the past two days. It was the very outcome Nilkanth had feared since the day he first learned Jayashree was expecting. The unspoken wound of inadequacy—the dread of losing his son to the city and his home to silence—tightened in his chest.

Vinayak sat frozen, glancing between his father and his mother-in-law, the weight of the moment sinking heavily on his shoulders. Savitri's lips tightened, her eyes narrowing ever so slightly as she reached instinctively to hold Seema's hand. The joy of new life was still there, yes—but now tinged with the quiet storm of an uncertain future.

Jayashree felt a sharp unease crawl through her chest as she listened to her mother's stern words. She knew Deepa could be overbearing, but this time her bluntness stung deeper—

because it wasn't entirely wrong. The thought of taking her newborn into a village still grappling with water scarcity sent a ripple of doubt through her. She lowered her eyes, ashamed, and glanced at Vinayak with a silent gesture of apology. Her heart ached—for him, for their love, and for the impossible choice placed before them.

Vinayak felt that glance like a weight on his chest. He said nothing, but inside, a quiet storm of helplessness churned. The joy of fatherhood now stood shadowed by the fear of watching his family drift apart—bit by bit, like cracked earth in a summer drought.

Across the room, Shankar watched them all—his wife's sharp tongue, his daughter's guilt, his son-in-law's silent anguish, and the quiet sorrow resting on Nilkanth and Savitri's faces. The room, just moments ago filled with sweetness and celebration, now sat under the heavy silence of a question none of them could answer:

Can love survive when water runs dry?

Vinayak drew in a shaky breath and lowered his gaze before speaking softly, his voice barely rising above a whisper, "Aai... I'll try to talk to my school management. Maybe they can approve a transfer near Pune. Until then, I'll come on weekends."

There was a long pause. The silence in the room grew deeper—almost too heavy to bear.

Then, turning to his father with hesitant eyes, Vinayak added, "Baba... I know this decision may hurt you. I know you were hoping for something else. But... Jayashree and the baby—

at this moment, they need comfort, safety... clean water. Maybe... when things improve, when the water returns... we'll come back."

Nilkanth sat frozen for a long moment. His hands trembled ever so slightly on his knees. The words from his son—the very son he raised with faith and fire, the son he imagined filling their home with new generations—had struck him like a gentle but merciless blow.

His eyes clouded with unwept tears, but his voice remained quiet and restrained. "Savitri," he said, slowly rising to his feet, "our son... he's become wiser than us. He's thinking of the future." He paused and looked toward the doorway. "We should leave now. Or else we'll miss the bus."

The quiet finality in his voice silenced the room.

Vinayak stood motionless, as if he'd just realized the weight of his own decision. His eyes pleaded for understanding, but his lips had no words left. Somewhere in that silent space between father and son, a thousand unsaid things hovered, aching to be spoken but buried beneath pride, responsibility, and time.

Savitri rose and held Seema's hand. Her heart burned, but she too wore a smile—not out of joy, but out of strength. She watched Nilkanth's retreating steps, her eyes aching with tears she couldn't shed in front of her son.

Seema walked over to Jayashree, who was seated, pale from childbirth and heartbreak. The young mother bent to touch her grandmother-in-law's feet, but Seema quickly pulled her into an embrace. "Stay blessed, my child," she whispered, brushing a trembling hand over Jayashree's hair. "We'll miss our prince."

Jayashree clutched her arm tightly, her lips trembling but silent. Her mother, Deepa, sat nearby, proud and unsentimental—but even she seemed briefly moved by the silence that wrapped the room like a winding shroud.

At the door, Shankar stepped forward and gently placed a hand on Nilkanth's shoulder. "Nilkanth… I know Vinayak's words may have cut deep. But I understand and I know this hurts. Don't let it turn into distance between us Vinayak must be worried due to the child. Please, come for naamkaran. Bring Savitri. Bring Mausi and Bhausahab. You all must come. I will call you."

Nilkanth managed a nod. But he didn't trust his voice anymore.

Vinayak quietly picked up their bags and walked behind his parents. His steps were heavy—burdened with guilt, and a longing that had nowhere to go.

Savitri didn't look back. Seema covered her mouth with her saree pallu, hiding her sobs. And Nilkanth? He kept his gaze steady ahead—but inside him, something fragile had cracked.

A father's silence.

A mother's sacrifice.

A son's helplessness.

A family pulled by love in opposite directions—one toward water, the other toward roots.

After around twenty-one days, the date for the naming ceremony was fixed.

The Joshi household in Pune was abuzz with preparations, yet far away, in the quiet courtyard of a Konkan village, Nilkanth sat absorbed in sculpting an idol—his fingers shaping devotion into form, his heart heavy and distracted.

Vinayak had returned to the village a week before to bring Savitri and Seema along with him to Pune. As the morning of their departure arrived, he once again approached his father with a hopeful plea.

Standing hesitantly at the threshold of the courtyard, Vinayak said, "Baba... we will be truly blessed if you come with us. Your presence matters more than anything."

Nilkanth didn't look up at first. His hands were deep in clay, shaping the arch of a deity's crown. A long silence stretched between them before he finally paused and spoke—his voice low but resolute.

"The day I can bring my grandson here to live, breathe, and grow happily in this house... that will be the day I meet him."

The words struck Vinayak like a stone. He blinked in disbelief. "Baba..." he whispered, but Nilkanth had already returned to his work—his face carved with pain he refused to show.

Vinayak stood frozen for a moment, then lowered his eyes and turned away. He left in silence, his heart stung by his father's unyielding pride. Inwardly, he couldn't help but mock the stubbornness—what if that day never comes? What if waiting becomes forever?

Since that moment, an invisible wall began to rise between the father and son. Neither had wronged the other, and yet, both were trapped in the quiet aftermath of love strained by reality. Their decisions—logical, responsible, even noble—became bricks in the wall that now divided them. One waited in solitude, carving idols and holding fast to hope. The other moved forward, balancing duty to his growing family with a silent ache he could not name.

And so, the gap grew—not out of anger, but from two hearts broken differently, yet equally.

As the guests arrived and the house filled with the warmth of celebration, Jayashree's eyes often wandered toward the door, hoping, perhaps foolishly, that Nilkanth might change his mind and arrive unannounced. But her hopes quietly faded.

The ceremony began. Panditji examined the birth chart, chanted a few verses, and looked up with a smile. "Auspicious letters suggest a divine name," he said.

Seema stepped forward, her eyes glistening. "Then I would like to name him Advait," she said softly, her voice trembling.

"Advait," Panditji repeated with approval. "A beautiful name. Meaning non-dual, complete, unique—like the Supreme."

Seema couldn't hold back her tears. She took the baby into her lap and called out gently, "Oh, my Advait, my little love..."

To everyone's wonder, the infant chuckled and looked straight at her. Laughter and joy rippled through the room as everyone came forward to bless the child.

Later, when the baby was peacefully playing in a small cradle wrapped in a soft blue cloth, Jayashree quietly stepped out onto the balcony. The noise of celebration softened behind her. Her fingers trembled slightly as she dialed Nilkanth's number.

The call connected.

"Baba..." Jayashree said, her voice slow but steady. "Jayashree here. How are you? How's Ajoba?"

From the other end came a warm, slow reply—tired, yet deeply affectionate.

"Oh, Jaya beti! We're fine... Just me and Baba sitting out in the courtyard. How are you? And how is our prince? Is the ceremony done?"

"Yes, Baba. We all missed you…" she said, holding back tears. "We named him Advait. Ajji chose the name. Panditji said it's perfect."

There was a pause, and then Nilkanth spoke—his voice softening with pride and meaning.

"Advait... what a powerful name. One-of-a-kind. Non-dual. Like Vishnu himself. May he grow into the wholeness his name carries. But beta, you both now carry a big responsibility. A soul has been entrusted to your care."

Jayashree broke down.

"But Baba... Advait's life... it will always feel incomplete without your blessings. Please... I know Vinayak said things that hurt you. I know you've built walls since that day, but don't let that moment come between you and your grandson. Please come. Forgive him. Forgive us."

There was silence.

Then Nilkanth spoke, slowly, like a sculptor smoothing the last curve of an idol.

"Beti, I was never angry. And I've already forgiven. But this distance... I chose it not out of hurt, but out of duty. I must prove that this village can survive—that water will never again drive a family apart. That when Advait comes here, he finds a future, not a struggle."

Jayashree wiped her tears and smiled faintly, understanding the love hidden beneath his sacrifice.

"Then Baba," she said, "your blessing has already reached him. And he will wait, like we all do, for the day his Ajoba takes him in his arms."

From the other end, Nilkanth whispered, barely audible—

"Tell him... tell him his Ajoba is waiting too."

Two months had passed since Advait's birth. His gentle coos and new expressions were the daily delight of both families. Around this time, Vinayak received a request-based transfer to a government school located in a village near Pune. To maintain balance, he rented a modest flat on the city outskirts but hadn't yet moved in, as classes remained online due to the looming second wave of the pandemic. For the time being, he stayed with Jayashree and Advait at her parents' home.

But back in the village, the absence of Vinayak had carved a silent, painful vacuum within the Jadhav home. The laughter had grown faint. The house, once bustling with rhythm and care, now echoed with stillness. Stress and solitude crept in like damp mist, triggering frailties in both Seema and Ramesh.

Then came the second wave of Covid—fiercer, deadlier. Within days, Seema and Ramesh both tested positive. Panic swept through the village, and the local administration sealed off the Jadhav house in quarantine. Savitri broke the news to Vinayak, her voice shaking, and soon the entire family found themselves drowning in dread.

When Ramesh's oxygen levels plummeted, Nilkanth didn't wait. He summoned an ambulance, praying against time, and rushed both parents to the district hospital. But like many others during that grim period, the hospital too was overwhelmed, its resources crumbling under the weight of the wave. Doctors tried, but quietly confessed the truth: there was nothing they could do.

Nilkanth stood in disbelief. The thought of losing both his parents in a single breath felt like being torn at the roots.

Savitri clung to hope. In a dim hospital corridor, she chanted Ganpati mantras under her breath, her rosary tightly clenched in her fist, her lips cracked from fasting.

But by the next morning, reality hit with a final blow. At 9 a.m., Ramesh slipped away. An hour later, Seema followed.

Two heartbeats silenced.
Two lifetimes gone.
Within the same stretch of breath.

Nilkanth collapsed into the chair outside the ICU. The hospital, bound by pandemic protocol, didn't allow the family to claim the bodies. From behind glass walls and masked faces, they watched the last rites being performed by hospital staff. No rituals, no farewell touch—just smoke, wind, and loss.

Something broke inside Nilkanth that day.

A sculptor who had once believed in shaping gods with love and devotion now stared blankly at the sky above the crematorium. His heart had turned into clay—wet, shapeless, trembling.

He cried out—not just in pain, but in protest.

"Why, Bappa? What sin did I commit? You took my parents… my son is gone… my grandson, too far from me. Am I being punished for the idols I made with faith? What more do you want from me?"

His sobs racked through his chest.

Savitri knelt beside him, her own tears falling silently. She placed a trembling hand on his head and whispered through her grief:

"Don't say that, Nilkanth. Don't break like this. Bappa hasn't forsaken us... he's testing us. If he has taken something away, he's preparing to return more—deeper, purer. I'm still here with you. You're not alone."

Nilkanth shook his head, his voice a whisper of anguish.

"But why these tests, Savitri? Why this cruelty?"

She looked up at the grey sky streaked with smoke and answered gently:

"You once told me that only when we break the hardest rocks deep beneath the earth, water flows. That only through breaking can something precious emerge. Perhaps this is what Bappa is doing—breaking our worldly attachments to awaken something greater in us."

Her voice wavered, but her conviction held.

"Aai and Baba... they are gone in body, yes. But they live in us. Their love, their teachings—they'll walk beside us every day."

Nilkanth slowly lifted his tear-streaked face, looked at her with a dawning clarity.

"Yes... breaking the stone brings water."

He held her hands in his trembling palms and said, more to himself than her—

"I must return to those words. I will not let their deaths go in vain. I will bring water to this village, and I will bring my grandson—Advait—home. Our home."

Savitri looked at him in still silence, her heart aching yet slowly stirring with hope. Nilkanth pulled her gently into his arms.

As they stepped out of the crematorium, the evening sun broke through the clouds. It wasn't warm, not yet. But it was light. And it followed them quietly—two grieving souls determined to rebuild.

Chapter 7

Back to present days of Hope

After a week of rain, the morning arrived wrapped in golden serenity. The sky, washed clean by the monsoon, gleamed softly as the sun filtered through the moist green canopy. Birds chirped cheerfully by the window sill, their little songs echoing like nature's prayer. The mild sunrays tiptoed through the faded curtains and gently caressed Nilkanth's closed eyelids, nudging him from sleep.

A sudden call from Savitri broke the lull.

"Nilkanth! It's already eight o'clock!"

His eyes snapped open. He fumbled for his mobile on the bedside table and gasped as he saw the time. "Eight?!" he murmured, almost in disbelief. It had been years since he had slept this long.

Throwing aside the thin quilt, he hurried to freshen up and stepped out, still tying the knot of his kurta.

In the kitchen, Savitri sat by the small wooden table, sunlight dancing on her silver-threaded hair. A steaming cup of tea sat beside the newspaper she was flipping through, her reading glasses slightly tilted on her nose. The kitchen was filled with the familiar scent of ginger and cardamom from the chai, mingling with the crisp freshness of the post-rain air.

She glanced at him and smirked gently.
"Finally, the great sculptor awakens," she teased, handing him his cup.

Nilkanth took it with a sheepish grin, settling into the chair across from her.

"I don't remember the last time I slept so much," he admitted, rubbing his eyes.

Savitri looked at him over her glasses. "It's a good sign," she said softly. "Maybe your heart has started healing… little by little."

Nilkanth didn't reply immediately. He stared into his tea, the steam curling up like faded memories. He could still feel the hollowness in the house—but the sun, the chirping birds, the warm tea, and Savitri's quiet company felt like stitches on a wound too wide to close, but slowly trying.

He finally spoke, his voice barely above a whisper.
"Savitri, I want to begin something new… For Advait."

Savitri's hand reached out, resting gently over his. With a wide, searching gaze, she asked softly,

"It's been two years since Vinayak left us, but you rarely speak of him or Advait. Not a word, not even a whisper... Though I know you remember them—just like I do. Is it because I mentioned last evening that Vinayak is coming for the Ganpati idol? Did that awaken something?"

Nilkanth looked at her and smiled faintly, his eyes glinting with memories.

"Savitri... last night, my entire life played out before me, frame by frame. And the one sentence you spoke... it kept ringing in my ears."

Savitri tilted her head, curious.

"What sentence? You remember what I said?"

He nodded. "Yes. That day at the cremation ground, when I was crumbling—you said, 'Just like strong rocks must be cut to bring water from the earth's depths, Bappa breaks us to bring out our true purpose.' That line... it hasn't left me."

Savitri's lips curved into a tender smile.

"Oh that? But I only repeated what I had learnt from you. Why has it stayed with you so strongly?"

Nilkanth's voice grew firmer now.

"Because, for the first time, I truly believe it. I feel it, Savitri. If I can carve idols from stone, shape gods from clay... why can't I also shape a future where water runs free in our village? Maybe I can... maybe we all can."

Savitri burst into laughter, gently mocking him, though her eyes softened.

"Oh ho! Listen to this—our clay idol-maker wants to challenge the engineers now? The same engineers who shook their heads and left saying, 'The rock layers here are too deep, too stubborn.' And you—who's never touched a drill—will solve it?"

She stood up, stretching slightly, wincing as her knees ached with age.

"Boss, enough with these grand dreams. It's Sunday. Go to the market and bring fresh vegetables—and fish, if there's good stock. I'll go collect the water before the queue gets longer."

Nilkanth lowered his eyes, jaw slackened—not in anger, but in quiet shame.That even now, Savitri—with aching knees and tired bones—must drag buckets from the community tap. That he, despite everything, couldn't ease her burden. Helplessness pooled inside him, thick and bitter.

As Savitri picked up the brass pot and headed to the door, he sat frozen at the table, her words echoing louder than she knew. But so did his own resolve—quiet, steady, and slowly rising like water from the depths of stubborn stone.

As Savitri walked toward the community tap, the morning sun already harsh on her shoulders, a pang of guilt tightened in her chest. Her words from earlier echoed in her ears—sharp, dismissive, thoughtless.

She hadn't meant to laugh at him, not really.

"He must be longing to see Advait more than anyone else," she thought, slowing her steps.

At their age, grandchildren were not just a source of joy—they were life's way of anchoring them to the world again, to hope, to legacy. Perhaps more than even she, Nilkanth had been dreaming of that tiny pair of hands gripping his finger, of watching his grandson toddle through the courtyard chasing butterflies.

"I shouldn't have scolded him like that," she sighed.

She had seen it—that flicker of hurt in his eyes when she teased him about his dream of bringing water to the village. Maybe it wasn't absurd after all. Maybe it was all he had left to hold on to—a purpose, a way to bring his fractured family back together.

By the time she returned, balancing two filled pots on her hips, sweat streaking her temples, she reached the doorstep and paused.

The house was latched from outside. Nilkanth must have gone to the market, she thought.

The next evening, Nilkanth returned home from the workshop with a strange gleam in his eyes—an excitement Savitri hadn't seen in years. His kurta was smudged with streaks of clay as usual, but his step carried a spring, and his smile lingered longer than usual.

Savitri, who was folding clothes in the hallway, paused and looked at him intently.

"Something's definitely up," she said, her eyebrows arching with curiosity. "It's been years since I've seen you return from work looking like a boy who found buried treasure. What's going on? Is there something special tomorrow?"

Nilkanth's smile widened, and he turned to her with a teasing glint in his eyes. "Savitri, are you omniscient now? Reading my mind like one of those sages in our old storybooks?"

Savitri chuckled, swatting his shoulder lightly with the towel in her hand. "When you've shared 35 years of your life with someone, you don't need divine powers. We resonate like two tanpuras tuned to the same pitch. I can sense your moods before even you know them."

Nilkanth mock-gasped and folded his hands in mock reverence. "So I've married a goddess, have I? I should probably start offering you flowers every morning."

Rolling her eyes and placing two cups of tea on the table, she laughed. "Flatter me all you want, but come to the point now. What's got you glowing like the sunrise? And don't you dare say it's nothing. Tomorrow's your birthday, isn't it?"

Nilkanth took the cup from her hands and sat down, his face softening. "It's nothing much, really. Some of my students have planned a picnic by the beach. They say they want to celebrate my birthday there—with some vada pav, songs, and salty breeze. They've asked me to bring you along too."

Savitri tilted her head and studied him for a moment, her smile warm. "So… the quiet birthday boy is finally letting the world sing for him?"

He shrugged, sheepish. "I never much liked celebrating my birthday. After a point, it just felt like a date on the calendar.

But… this year, I don't know, something feels different. Maybe I've been waiting for a reason to feel alive again."

Savitri's eyes softened as she reached out and placed a hand over his. "Then let's go to the beach, Nilkanth. Let's feel alive again together.

The next morning, Savitri rose earlier than usual. The sky was still a pale lavender, and the cool breeze carried the gentle rustle of leaves. Quietly, she walked to the Vinayak temple at the edge of the village, her heart heavy with a prayer she had never voiced aloud before—not just for Nilkanth's health, but for the ache in his heart to be healed.

Standing before the idol of Ganesha, her hands folded and eyes closed, she whispered, "Bappa, today is his birthday. Please give him what no medicine ever can. Let him hear the laughter of his grandson, feel his little arms around his neck… bring Advait home."

After the darshan, she returned and went straight to the kitchen. The aroma of fried snacks—chakli, kothimbirvadi, and crisp karanjis—soon filled the air, blending with the comforting scent of ginger tea.

Nilkanth, still rubbing the sleep from his eyes, entered the kitchen and was surprised to see the spread. As he reached for his cup, Savitri bent down to touch his feet.

He gently stopped her mid-bow and pulled her into a sudden, tight embrace.

She blinked rapidly, her eyes damp. "Happy birthday, my hero," she said softly, voice catching. "You know… this morning

I told Bappa that next year, we must celebrate your birthday with Advait by our side."

Nilkanth pulled back, staring at her with gentle astonishment. "How do you always know?" he murmured, his voice thick. "Yes, Savitri… I made a silent promise to myself. Before the next Ganeshotsav, I will bring them back. Advait deserves to know this home… and I deserve to hear him call me 'Ajoba'."

Savitri placed a hand over his chest and smiled through her tears. "He will, Nilkanth. He will. Bappa is listening. He's just waiting for the right moment."

They stood there for a long while, wrapped not just in each other's arms, but in the quiet, resilient hope that had always carried them through storms.

Nilkanth typed out a message with his usual care, glasses sliding to the tip of his nose:

"All students assemble near the workshop by 10. We'll walk to the beach together for the picnic."

Savitri, meanwhile, stood in the bedroom holding a neatly folded shirt—a soft, off-white half-sleeve with a delicate grey textured print. She had handpicked the cloth weeks ago, quietly stitching it in the afternoons when Nilkanth was at his workshop.

As he came out of the washroom, she held it up to him with a smile that carried years of love.

"Here's your birthday shirt, freshly stitched by your old tailor."

Nilkanth held it up in surprise, rubbing the fabric gently. "Oh ho! Beautiful lady, you made this old chap look like a newlywed groom today."

Savitri blushed and turned away, pretending to adjust her jasmine garland. "Well, you're accompanying a pageant today, remember? So you had to look the part."

He laughed softly, came closer, and tucked the jasmine bloom firmly into her braid. "A pageant? She's no less than a queen. My queen. My heartthrob since I had black hair and no belly."

She rolled her eyes, but the smile wouldn't leave her face. The warmth in his words made her forget the pain in her knees and the ache of years.

Savitri packed the snacks she had lovingly prepared—batata vadas, poha chivda, and her special coconut peda. On their way, she stopped to buy pedhas and jalebis from the local sweet shop, tucking them carefully in a bag alongside steel tumblers and paper napkins.

As they neared the workshop, a loud cheer erupted—
"Happy Birthday, Sir! We wish you a hundred more!"

All eighteen of his students stood with wide grins, some holding small handmade cards and garlands. Their joy was pure, their respect heartfelt. For a moment, Nilkanth stood frozen, overcome by a swell of emotion. His eyes moistened as he looked at Savitri, silently thanking her for making this day special—yet again.

These were not just students anymore. Over the past year, Nilkanth's little workshop had transformed into something larger. With the support of a retired colleague and a few officials from the state education department, he had applied for and finally received affiliation from the University of Mumbai, allowing him to offer a certified course in Fine Arts—focusing on traditional idol-making, clay modelling, and mural design.

Now, his students wouldn't just learn with their hands—they would walk away with a university-accredited certificate that could open doors for them: as artists, designers, or teachers in schools and NGOs. For a man who once carved Ganesha with only the blessings of his ancestors, this was no less than a personal revolution.

He cleared his throat and extended his gratitude to all the students with folded hands and began handing out sweets, each with a personal word, a blessing, a smile.

He then lifted his bag, took Savitri's hand, and nodded.
"Let's go! The waves are waiting."

And just like that, the unlikely pageant began—eighteen young students, a beloved teacher, and his queen—all walking down the sun-dappled lane toward the beach, where laughter would echo, feet would dip into sand, and for a little while, everything broken in the world would feel whole again.

Among all the students, the youngest was little Janvi, a bright-eyed girl from class five. She clutched Savitri's hand tightly and began chatting with a childlike mix of innocence and enthusiasm.

"Madam! You know, my Ajji must be as old as you," she said, peering up at Savitri. "But she's not this active. She has a heart problem and mostly stays in bed. But you—you're so healthy and strong! I like you a lot. Will you tell me stories once we reach the beach? Will you play with me?"

Before Savitri could answer, Janvi added with a sigh, "These elder students never let me in their teams to play."

Savitri smiled and softly ran her fingers over the girl's hair. "No worries, my sweetheart. Today, you are in my team. We'll play with the waves and build castles in the sand."

That brought a wide grin to Janvi's face. Holding Savitri's hand more tightly, she skipped a little as she walked and continued, "My Ajoba passed away a few weeks ago… he was my best friend. I used to play with him every evening. I miss him so much."

Those words—"Ajoba passed away"—fell like a chisel's blow on Nilkanth's heart, was walking silently beside them. He flinched, though he didn't stop. The ache of Seema and Ramesh's absence stirred afresh, as did the distance from his own grandson.

Then came the question that cracked his heart open.

"Madam, don't you have any grandchildren?"

Savitri, quick to sense Nilkanth's hurt, gently squeezed his hand behind her back and replied to Janvi with a soft smile:

"Oh yes, I do! His name is Advait. He's about three years old now, lives in Pune."

Janvi's eyes widened, sparkling with excitement. "Three?! Oh! He must be very cute, Madam! I love babies! If he were here today, I would've played with him all day long. Sir, when will Advait come?"

She looked up at Nilkanth with hopeful eyes. He hesitated for a second, the edges of his smile tight with emotion, but Savitri stepped in, her voice warm:

"He'll come soon, beta... very soon."

The group soon reached the sea beach, where waves greeted them with the rhythmic thunder of reunion. Students scattered with joy, removing their sandals, chasing each other along the edge of the water.

Savitri stood silently near the shoreline, watching the endless blue. Her saree fluttered gently in the salty breeze. Nilkanth walked up and stood beside her, not saying a word.

She looked at the water and murmured, "Do you remember this place?"

Nilkanth nodded faintly, his eyes fixed on the horizon.

"Yes... we came here after Vinayak's wedding. Just the two of us.

Savitri smiled, her eyes moist.

"Back then, we had never thought that we both will remain alone."

Nilkanth looked at the children playing, Janvi waving at him in the distance, and said under his breath,

"I have made up my mind, Savitri. I will bring our Advait home."

Savitri turned to him, eyes shining like wet sand under morning sun.

"Yes, you will. And I will wait, just like I always have."

Together, they watched the waves rise and fall, like the tides of time that had brought them here—older, lonelier perhaps—but still tethered by love, by purpose, and now, by the promise of a return.

By the time they reached the shore together, little Janvi was already busy sculpting shapes in the soft sand with her tiny hands, completely engrossed in her own world. Nilkanth scanned the beach and noticed that his students had scattered in different directions, laughing and playing near the water.

Raising his voice just enough to carry over the sea breeze, he called out their names one by one. Within moments, the obedient bunch came jogging back towards him, sand clinging to their feet and joy dancing in their eyes.

"Listen carefully, everyone," Nilkanth said, his voice both firm and fatherly. "It's already ten. Make sure none of you wander too far from here. I'll keep an eye on everyone—especially Suresh and Mohan," he added with a teasing smile, which made the two boys grin sheepishly.

He pointed to a small eatery along the road by the shore. "We'll head there for lunch around twelve. So no matter what you're doing, be back here by then, alright?"

All the students nodded enthusiastically, and the little group dispersed again like happy birds, each to their patch of beach, carrying laughter with them.

Nilkanth was watching little Janvi with quiet fondness, her small fingers busy shaping the sand into a miniature world of her own. He spread a mat at a comfortable distance from her and gestured Savitri to sit. The couple settled down – Nilkanth slipped in his earphones to listen to a soothing Panduranga Abhanga, while Savitri pulled out her ball of wool and knitting needles. She had started making a warm, soft cap – a special gift for Advait.

A serene silence fell between them, broken only by the rhythmic crashing of waves and the innocent chatter of Janvi, who continued speaking to herself, lost in storytelling as she sculpted her sand palace. Her voice floated toward them like a tune from childhood.

Nilkanth smiled, eyes soft with affection. "Janvi! Whatever you're building, I'm going to come inspect it the moment you finish. So be sure to call me, alright?"

Savitri looked up from her knitting, her face warm with a smile. "Yes, Janvi! I want to see it too. Don't forget us!"

Nilkanth waved a gentle hand, half-laughing. "If we call them now, they'll get irritated. Let them enjoy for a while—when they get hungry, they'll come to us on their own. Let's give them some more time."

Savitri chuckled and returned to her knitting, and Nilkanth leaned back, closing his eyes as the soothing abhangas played on. Above them, the clouds shifted lazily, and beside them, Janvi's small voice carried the laughter of a child who unknowingly brought warmth to two aching hearts.

Suddenly, Janvi walked over with her sweet, chirpy voice and asked,

"Madam! Were you saying something about snacks? What special treats have you brought for us today?"

Savitri smiled, amused by her endearing demand. Her eyes softened as she replied,

"Yes, I did bring something special. But first, go clean your hands and then come sit with us. I'll serve you, my little guest."

Janvi nodded obediently and quickly went to wash her sandy hands. As soon as she sat cross-legged beside Savitri and began munching on the snacks, the aroma must have reached the others. In no time, the rest of the students came running, their eyes wide and eager.

"Madam! We're hungry too!" they chorused, half-laughing.

Savitri laughed heartily, her heart full.

"Come, come! There's enough for everyone. Here—take the box and share among yourselves."

She handed the large container to the students, who quickly and joyfully helped themselves, passing it around with cheerful gratitude. Laughter and chatter echoed softly across the beach as they devoured the homemade treats.

Nilkanth sat back quietly, his gaze fixed on Savitri. There was a deep contentment in his eyes as he watched her glow in the happiness of being surrounded by young hearts and grateful smiles. Her joy today was like the sun—bright, generous, and golden.

For a brief moment, Nilkanth felt a quiet completeness.

But deep inside, a small ache remained.

This was perhaps one of the most blissful birthdays he'd ever experienced—unexpected, tender, and meaningful in every sense. Yet the one thing that would have made it truly whole was missing: his son, his Jayashree, and their little Advait.

That absence clung to the edge of his joy, like a shadow at sunset.

He looked out at the sea, the waves folding endlessly into each other, and silently prayed that someday soon, the waves would bring them all home again.

After the snack break, the beach came alive once again. Some students raced toward the waves, laughter echoing as they splashed and played. A few of the boys, having brought extra clothes, dove gleefully into the sea, their silhouettes dancing in the sunlight.

Meanwhile, the clock struck 12 noon, and Nilkanth rose from the mat, dusting off the sand. His eyes scanned the shoreline, counting each of his students with the gentle attentiveness of a father.

As his gaze landed on Janvi, he noticed her standing beside her sand structure with hands on her hips, studying it with intense focus. She looked like a little engineer inspecting her masterpiece before inviting her teacher for approval.

Nilkanth called out, smiling,

"Are you ready, Janvi? Shall I come see now?"
Janvi turned, her eyes sparkling,
"Yes, Sir! Please come! Madam, you too!" she chirped.

Nilkanth and Savitri walked over and were instantly struck by what they saw. There, molded carefully out of sand, stood a regal palace, complete with turrets, gates, and—most curiously—a shaft like well, detailed with tiny steps crawling downward.

Janvi, glowing with pride, began explaining animatedly,
"Here's the palace entrance. The king comes through this gate. His guards fetch water from the well using these steps. See? Even in summer, they don't run out!"

Savitri was charmed—more by Janvi's innocent storytelling than the sculpture itself. But somewhere in that play, a hidden truth shone through.
She thought quietly: Even a child knows that access to water is power. Even she dreams of a well with stairs… that never runs dry.

But Nilkanth, though standing beside them, was no longer there. His eyes were locked on the well Janvi had shaped—but his mind had drifted far, tumbling through memories, thoughts, forgotten research… and then—

A thunderbolt of an idea struck him.

His eyes widened. His breath caught. He bent down suddenly and swept Janvi up into his arms, spinning her gently in a circle.

"Janvi!" he said, his voice vibrant, moved.

"I'm so proud of you today. You've no idea what you've done—but soon, you will. A miracle, child… you've just sparked a miracle."

Janvi blinked in surprise, unsure what miracle he meant, but grinning at the sudden praise.

Savitri's heart was full, but her mind echoed with one word: "Miracle?" She tilted her head, watching Nilkanth with a quiet intensity. Something had changed in him—there was purpose in his eyes again. Had he… really found a clue to the water crisis?

Nilkanth knelt down, pulled out his phone, and snapped photos of the sand sculpture from multiple angles. A few taps later, he shared them in their student group with a message:

"Art that can inspire change—Janvi's model may hold the key to a new beginning. Look closely."

Then he turned and pulled a chocolate bar from his pocket, offering it to Janvi.

"This," he said, "is your award for building something that just might change the fate of this entire village."

Janvi accepted it with wide eyes, still unsure why her little castle had stirred so much excitement.

But Savitri watched her husband closely, the rising breeze stirring her hair, her heart both anxious and hopeful.

She knew him well. He wasn't just moved by a child's drawing—he had seen a solution in the innocence of sand well.

With the sun climbing high, Nilkanth called out for the students and gathered the group. After counting them one by one, he waved toward the roadside restaurant.

"Let's go for lunch!" he announced, still smiling like a man reborn.

Yet only Savitri noticed—the smile on his face was not just from joy.

It was the smile of a man who had found his purpose again.

Savitri had been quietly observing Nilkanth ever since he saw Janvi's sand palace. Though he moved with the group to the restaurant, joined in their laughter, and stood among them, his mind clearly wandered elsewhere—his eyes glazed, his silence deeper than usual.

The students, having planned a small surprise, gathered around and presented a homemade cake.

They sang "Happy Birthday, Sir!" they cheered, forming a circle.

Nilkanth smiled faintly and cut the cake as everyone clapped and sang. The children cheered, fed him the first slice, and joyfully served themselves. Savitri too joined in, savoring every bit of the meal, grateful for the brightness these students brought into their otherwise quiet life.

Nilkanth ordered Pav Bhaji, soon they were served garnished creatively with grated cheese and coriander along with chilled butter milk which was relaxing for a sunny noon.

But Nilkanth only nibbled at his food. His gaze drifted beyond the shoreline, his ears deaf to the chatter around him. He was elsewhere—caught in a whirl of thoughts too intense to speak aloud.

After lunch, while the students gathered to go home, Nilkanth quietly called four of his senior students aside—Suresh, Mohan, Prashant, and Pankaj.

In a low, determined voice, he said,

"This evening at 7, meet me at my house. We need to start a project… something big. Don't tell the others yet. It's important and confidential. "

The boys, sensing the seriousness in his tone, nodded without asking too many questions.

On the way back home, as the sun began its slow descent and golden light filled the village path, Savitri walked beside Nilkanth in silence, holding the empty tiffin and leftover snack box.

She finally broke the silence, her tone soft, almost casual:

"I'll arrange dinner for your boys. Don't forget to remind them. I'll clear Vinayak's old study table so you five can sit together and work comfortably."

Nilkanth stopped in his tracks for a moment and looked at her.

"You read my mind again, didn't you?" he asked with a faint smile.

Savitri grinned, looking sideways with mock pride.

"Of course. Thirty-five years, Nilkanth. I've had enough time to learn your silences better than your words."

She paused, then teased him lightly,

"I'll even keep your well in my prayers tonight to Bappa... who knows, Bappa might just grant your wish."

Nilkanth laughed softly, touched by her words and the gentle faith she never let go of. His eyes shimmered—not with grief, but with the quiet fire of purpose reborn.

Chapter 8

Dreams took a Real Shape

The four boys—Suresh, Mohan, Prashant, and Pankaj—had all completed their graduation and shared a common dream: to make idol-making their profession and continue living in their native village. Each of them came from humble backgrounds, but their determination to stay rooted and contribute meaningfully to the craft bound them together.

Suresh and Mohan were cousin brothers who lived under the same roof in a joint family. Tall, well-built, and often brimming with false pride about their physique, the duo was locally known more as "bodyguards". Their popularity among girls was more for their protective nature than any romantic charm—largely because they were usually penniless and humble in their means.

Prashant, the son of a farmer, had endured more than his fair share of hardship. He lost his father during the Covid pandemic, and his mother, now the sole breadwinner, worked tirelessly as a contract nurse at the district hospital. Despite his circumstances, Prashant shone with a natural brilliance. A science student with a sharp mind for calculations and measurements, he combined precision with passion, making him a standout artist in Nilkanth's eyes. Nilkanth saw in him the spark of a true successor, someone worthy of inheriting his legacy. Eager to blend tradition with innovation, Prashant enrolled in night classes for computer literacy, diving deep into digital design tools and 3D printing techniques. His dream was to create precision molds that could modernize the process of fiber-reinforced polymer (FRP) idol-making—adding value without compromising artistry.

And then there was Pankaj—the quietest and perhaps the most resilient of them all. Orphaned at a young age, he was raised in an ashram on the village outskirts. Every day, without fail, he came to the workshop, his eyes lit with hunger to learn and hands slowly shaping into those of a craftsman. He had no family, but in Nilkanth's humble space, he found mentorship, belonging, and a purpose that stitched his otherwise scattered world together.

Nilkanth often looked at the four boys not just as students, but as the future of the village's artistic soul—each one carrying a different thread, weaving together a new beginning.

After returning from the birthday picnic, Nilkanth had been quietly engrossed with his sketchbook, pencil, and a few old reference books all afternoon. Savitri, growing slightly irritated by his intense focus, came into the room holding a tray with two cups of tea and a glass of water. As she placed them on the table, she reminded him firmly, "Enough of your sketches now. The boys will be here any moment. Go freshen up."

But Nilkanth looked up, his eyes glowing with excitement. "Savitri, wait—let's have our tea here. I want to show you something before anyone else sees it. You must understand and approve it first."

Savitri paused, her curiosity piqued despite her irritation. "Why tea here, all of a sudden?" she asked, frowning a little as she walked over.

Nilkanth grinned. "Because without the approval of my home ministry, how can I launch this project?"

Savitri laughed out loud at the unexpected sweetness in his tone. "So now you're mocking me again, hmm? Fine, Mr. Visionary—, what is it that you've been cooking up in that head of yours?"

Savitri gently set the tea cups aside and leaned in, turning the pages of the sketchbook one by one. Her eyes followed each careful line, noticing how Nilkanth had developed Janvi's sand structure into something far more refined—there was precision now, a plan taking shape. But as she examined the drawings, a shadow of worry crept into her expression. A silent doubt stirred within her, one she hesitated to voice.

Nilkanth, ever attuned to her thoughts, caught it in her eyes. He smiled and said softly, "You're about to ask—how will I make this possible, right?" He paused, letting the silence speak for both of them, then continued with quiet resolve, "Savitri, we have over 366 days before the next Ganpati festival. If we give it our all—our hearts, our time, our hands—then what seems impossible today can be made possible."

Soon, a series of quick knocks echoed at the door. Savitri, wiping her hands on her sari, murmured as she rushed to answer, "Oh! The boys must be here. You finish your tea—I'll let them in."

Outside stood Suresh, Mohan, Prashant, and Pankaj, slightly nervous but smiling. They greeted Savitri politely. "Namaskar, Madam. Is Sir home?"

From inside, Nilkanth's voice rang out warmly, "Come in, boys!"

Savitri stepped aside and welcomed them in. This was the first time the boys had been invited into Nilkanth's home informally—outside of the usual festival celebrations like Shimgotsav or Ganeshotsav. The unexpected invitation, especially in the evening, made them uneasy.

Suresh whispered nervously to Mohan, "I think Sir found out about our teasing Kiran the other day."

Mohan smirked, nudging him, "You're always the one caught red-handed."

Just then, Nilkanth cleared his throat—firm and loud, immediately silencing them. The boys straightened up, standing in a line.

He looked at each of them, his gaze serious but calm. "I've called you here for a reason—an important one," he said. "There's a project I want us five to work on together. It's for the good of the village—your people, your families, your future. But before I tell you anything further, there's one condition."

The boys listened intently.

"You must not speak of this to anyone. No parents. No siblings. Not even your closest friends or classmates maintain absolute secrecy. This stays between us five—until I say otherwise. Only then will I reveal the plan."

The boys exchanged quick glances. There was no doubt in their minds—Nilkanth Sir had been more than a teacher to them. His words, his wisdom, his dedication—they trusted him as they did no one else. Without hesitation, they nodded.

And then, together, with conviction in their voices, they said in unison,

"Sir, we agree. We promise—no word will leave this room."

Nilkanth gestured for the boys to sit around the old wooden table, pulling out four chairs from the corners of the room. He himself sat cross-legged on the bed, his sketchpad and a stack of official-looking papers beside him. The evening light filtered through the window, casting soft amber shadows on the wall.

He opened a folded sheet—a detailed coordinate map marked with notations and color gradients. "This," he began, gently flattening the paper on the table, "is a geological survey map of our village."

The boys leaned forward, curiosity in their eyes. Nilkanth continued, "I got this from a friend—he's the Block Development Officer. This map was created using satellite imaging and ground surveys. The shades here," he pointed at the map, "indicate groundwater presence, depth, and flow density."

Prashant, ever sharp with science and detail, quickly started reading the gradients and numbers, his eyes scanning the legend. "Sir, these deep blue spots... they suggest higher water retention, don't they?"

Nilkanth smiled. "Exactly. And look here—one of the points they marked," he paused, pointing to a spot on the middle of the village, "is right beside our house. Decades ago, there used to be a well there. It dried up long before your time. But I remember it. We all do."

The room grew quiet. Each of the boys, now fully attentive, could sense the gravity in his voice.

Nilkanth leaned forward, voice steady but filled with determination. "I showed you this map not just to share a dream, but to help you believe. The project we start today will be rooted in facts. Science is guiding us—but we will carve the way with our hands."

The boys took notes silently, some exchanging looks of excitement.

Nilkanth continued, his eyes focused, his tone now charged with a quiet fire. "We're going to reopen that well. We'll cut through rock layers that scared away machines and officials. But we won't be reckless—we'll do it with thought, planning, and innovation."

Suresh raised his hand hesitantly. "Sir… are you saying we'll dig it ourselves?"

Nilkanth nodded. "Yes. Not just with shovels and picks. I have something in mind—something creative. We'll design a structure to support our digging, monitor progress, and ensure safety. We'll use both traditional and modern ideas. What we're attempting isn't just labor—it's craft. And maybe… a little prayer too."

Mohan whispered under his breath, awestruck, "Sir… this is like digging a future out of stone."

Nilkanth looked at each of them, and finally said, "You're not just my students now. You're my comrades. We owe this to the land that raised us, and to the children who must not grow up thirsty."

Savitri, standing quietly at the door with a soft smile, had heard every word. She stepped in and placed a hand on Nilkanth's shoulder. "Let's bring water back to our soil," she said simply. "And with it, our family too."

That very evening, Nilkanth laid out a detailed, month-wise plan for the entire project. Each phase—survey, excavation, reinforcement, and testing—was charged with timelines and fallback options. The room buzzed with the quiet excitement of a new beginning.

From the next day itself, the first phase was to begin: securing the site. They decided to enclose the area near the old well with tarpaulin sheets, erecting a tent-like structure to conceal and protect their work. It would also serve to keep curious villagers at bay.

As the group reviewed the final preparations, Savitri, standing with a folded shawl in her arms, raised a practical concern.

"But tomorrow morning, Vinayak is coming, isn't he? He'll be here to collect the Ganpati idol. What will you say to him when he sees all this going on?"

Nilkanth paused for a second, then gave a calm but firm smile. "Only if I let him stay long enough to notice. Within two days, Ganpati festival begins, and so does our project. He'll have to rush back to Pune."

Savitri looked at him in surprise, registering the steely resolve in his eyes. For a moment, she was startled—was Nilkanth really placing the project above the time he could spend with his son? But then the truth dawned quietly on her.

She realized it wasn't disregard—it was devotion.

This wasn't just a project to dig a well. It was his way of building a path—not only for water, but to bring Vinayak back. Forever. To make the village worthy of his return. To gift him a legacy deeper than the idols they molded—a living, breathing connection to the soil he once left behind.

Savitri softened, a sigh escaping her lips. She tucked the shawl under her arm and said gently, "You're not just digging a well, Nilkanth. You're digging for your family and the entire village."

Nilkanth didn't respond in words. He simply looked out of the window, where the moonlight had begun to spill over the courtyard—silent, sacred, and waiting.

The next morning, as Vinayak stepped into his childhood home, a wave of familiar warmth engulfed him. The scent of damp earth from the courtyard plants, the rustle of coconut fronds, and the faint fragrance of agarbatti hanging in the air—all pulled him deep into nostalgia.

The front door stood ajar, just as it used to when he was a boy coming back from school. He gently pushed the curtain aside and entered. On the center table, neatly packed and adorned with fresh garlands, stood the Ganapati idol—ready for departure.

Behind it, Savitri sat on the sofa with surprising ease, knitting in her lap, a calm smile on her face.

For a moment, Vinayak paused. Since the last two years, he had grown used to the delays, the hushed tensions, and the unspoken strain between his parents. Never had he seen the idol so neatly packed, ready, waiting—as if the house itself had prepared for his brief arrival and departure.

Savitri looked up. "Oh! Come, beta," she greeted him with genuine warmth. "Hope the journey was comfortable? How are Jayashree and Advait? They must be alone now? You should leave soon after lunch."

Her words were light, but her intentions clear—she was gently nudging him not to linger too long. Vinayak noticed the shift. His eyes, meanwhile, scanned the room, subtly searching for his father.

Savitri caught the glance. Her voice softened. "Your Baba just stepped out to the market. He wanted to buy your favorite coconut biscuits and some sweets for Advait. He should be back soon."

Vinayak managed a faint smile and stepped forward to touch her feet.

"I'll bring you a cup of tea," she said, rising. "Freshen up, beta. Lunch will be ready in a bit."

What she didn't say was that Nilkanth wasn't just out buying biscuits. He had taken Suresh with him to Ratnagiri, heading straight to the hardware store to collect precision tools and measuring equipment—last-minute essentials before launching the project that now consumed his heart and mind.

Around lunchtime, Nilkanth returned from the market, a shopping bag swinging lightly in his hand. As he stepped into the house, Vinayak glanced at him from the hallway—and immediately noticed the dried mud clinging to the bottom of his trousers.

His brow furrowed. It hasn't rained in days… he thought. Where could Baba have been to get mud on his clothes?

But he said nothing. Instead, he quickly approached and bent to touch Nilkanth's feet.

"Hope you all are well and in good health," Nilkanth said, placing a hand on his son's head. His tone was even, though a little hurried. "You start your meal—I'll join you in a few minutes."

With that, he slipped past into the kitchen, still carrying the bag. Once inside, he leaned in and whispered to Savitri, "Has he said when he'll leave? Did he go near the garden at the back?"

Savitri's eyes widened. She turned quickly, checking to make sure Vinayak wasn't nearby, then hushed him—"Yes, I told him. He'll be leaving soon. Don't worry—he hasn't noticed anything."

Nilkanth gave a brief nod of relief and set the bag down. "Let me pack the sweets and snacks for Advait," Savitri added, already reaching for the containers.

He gently patted her back, a quiet gesture of gratitude, and then hurried off to the washroom to clean up.

As she watched him disappear down the hall, Savitri shook her head with an affectionate sigh and muttered under her breath, smiling—"Truly, this man is mad."

Vinayak felt a strange sense of relief wash over him. His father's behavior—the same distant composure, the same quiet urgency—was exactly how he remembered it from that day years ago, the day he had refused to return to the village. Nothing had changed, and perhaps that, in some odd way, was comforting.

He turned to his mother, casually picking up on something he had overheard.

"Aai… why did you call Baba just now?"

Savitri, caught off guard but quick to recover, chuckled softly as she bent to arrange the utensils. She spoke with the practiced ease of a mother who had spent a lifetime weaving gentle half-truths.

"Oh, Beta?" she said, waving her hand dismissively. "Because of his childish nature. Imagine—crossing all that mud just to get 'Kele Halvo' from Kalyani Ajji's house for you. I never even asked him, but he remembered it's your favorite."

Vinayak's eyes lit up. He almost leapt in his seat.

"Aai! Really? Kele Halvo that heavenly sweet dish from Kalyani Ajji? Please, give me one now!"

Savitri smiled, both at his excitement and at the success of her little story. The truth, of course, was far simpler—she had gone to Kalyani Ajji's herself the previous day, knowing Vinayak would be thrilled. But if a harmless story kept her son from asking more questions, it was worth telling.

She handed him a piece, wrapped neatly in banana leaf.

"Here," she said warmly. "Store them properly in the fridge as soon as you reach home. If Advait doesn't gobble them all, they'll easily last you two weeks."

Vinayak took a bite and closed his eyes in delight.

Savitri watched him quietly, her smile lingering, even as her thoughts flickered briefly to Nilkanth and the secret that had already begun to take root.

Savitri had set the lunch table with care, each dish lovingly prepared, each plate arranged just so. When they all sat down together—Vinayak, Savitri, and Nilkanth—it felt like a fleeting glimpse of a time long gone.

Vinayak's face lit up as he saw the spread. "Aai! All my favorites?"

Savitri smiled as she served him. "Of course. Eat now, while it's still warm."

Vinayak began with enthusiasm, savoring each bite. But across the table, Nilkanth seemed lost—his fingers absentmindedly rolling a bit of rice, his gaze fixed on a glass of water as if trying to measure it with his eyes. He was deep in thought, mentally calculating something far from the dining table.

Savitri noticed and quickly interjected before Vinayak could comment. "So… how are your in-laws? They must be well? And Advait—he must be talking non-stop now! I heard him the other day when Jayashree called."

Vinayak chuckled. "Oh, Aai, he's a complete chatterbox now! As for Jayashree's parents, they're fine. Her mother drops in often. But Aai…"—his tone dropped—"I don't know how long I can keep up with the politics at the school. It's getting difficult."

Nilkanth, though seemingly distant, caught that line. Without looking up, he said in a quiet but firm tone, "Then come back to your old school. You'll have to next year anyway."

The words landed heavily. Savitri blinked, stunned. Vinayak looked at his father, surprised—his tone sounded less like a suggestion and more like a prophecy.

Savitri quickly stepped in to soften the air. She looked at Vinayak and smiled, gently brushing the topic with her voice, "Your father is always trying to find some excuse to bring you back. He misses you all more than he admits."

Vinayak gave a small smile. "Even we miss being here, Aai. Every day. But the water issue… it's what keeps us away."

Nilkanth's eyes flickered, and he inhaled sharply, about to speak.

But Savitri, anticipating him, kicked him lightly under the table.

He flinched and quickly busied himself with the food.

Savitri sighed and added, her voice laced with dramatic hope, "Yes, your father and the villagers are still pushing the BDO for help. Maybe Bappa will bless us with a miracle this year."

Vinayak glanced at his watch and gave a soft groan. "Aai, I should pack up. There's a bus at 4:30—it'll be easier to travel with the Ganpati idol in daylight."

Savitri felt a familiar heaviness settle in her chest. She nodded, hiding the ache behind her motherly smile. "Yes, that's better. It's not safe to travel late, especially carrying Bappa with you."

As she began to clear the table, the quiet between them lingered—each carrying more than what was said aloud.

Vinayak emerged from his room, dressed and ready, a quiet solemnity in his steps. The soft afternoon light filtered through the curtains, casting golden patterns on the floor. He walked slowly towards the center table where the little Ganpati idol rested, wrapped in a saffron cloth, cradled in silence.

With reverent hands, he lifted the idol onto his lap. For a moment, he just held it close, as if feeling the heartbeat of clay against his chest. Then, gently, almost like uncovering a newborn, he peeled back the cloth to catch a glimpse of Bappa's face.

The moment the idol's eyes met his—carved with such grace, such divine calm—a wave surged through him. There was softness in those eyes, a silent knowing, a kindness too vast to belong to this world. Vinayak's breath caught in his throat. His vision blurred. Tears welled up and spilled freely, as if the dam of years—of guilt, love, distance, and longing—had suddenly broken.

He whispered, his voice trembling like a prayer caught in the wind,

"Oh Bappa… bless this village. Gift the water of heaven to every house. And bring us back… bring us home."

From the far end of the veranda, behind the bamboo curtain, Nilkanth stood silently—unmoving, unnoticed. His eyes, sunken with years of quiet resolve, now brimmed with a flood he could no longer hold back. His fingers tightened around the pillar as tears ran down his weathered cheeks—not of sorrow, but of something far deeper. A father's pride. A sculptor's calling. A devotee's surrender.

In that silent moment, Nilkanth knew—with unshakable clarity—that this was no longer just a project. It was a vow. A sacred duty passed on by the very hands that had shaped Ganpati for forty-five years. The clay, the water, the prayers—they were all calling him to restore the soul of the village, to summon back the river beneath the rock.

And he would answer. With every breath left in him, he would answer.

Nilkanth came rushing as if he was busy somewhere else and rushed to kitchen to check whether Savitri was ready with all food packets and boxes. Savitri looking at him could make out his emotional turbulence while son is leaving. She made herself stronger enough to sallow down the intense environment calm down, so she entered with tray with tea and coconut cookies and said-"It's now 3.30 let's have the tea and your Baba will drop you to the bus stand. Good that the food packets and boxes all adjusted in your back sack bag."

About half an hour later, Nilkanth quietly stepped out of the house with Vinayak, carrying the idol with utmost care, both father and son walking side by side yet wrapped in their own silence. The road to the bus stand was quiet, shaded by the memory of old tamarind and gulmohar trees, each footstep echoing with unspoken words and the weight of love long buried beneath time and pride.

Back at home, Savitri stood still at the threshold, her hand resting lightly on the rusted gate, her eyes locked onto the path ahead—where the street slowly bent out of sight into the heart of the village. She didn't wave. She didn't call out. She just stood there, watching, waiting—until the figures of her son and husband became silhouettes, then shadows, then simply... gone.

Yet something stirred inside her—a quiet tremor of hope. Not loud or dramatic, but real and pulsing like a song long forgotten.

She looked up at the old guava tree where two parrots flitted noisily between the leaves, and smiled faintly. A strange warmth spread through her chest. A sense of faith.

"Soon," she whispered to herself, "soon, this house will echo with Advait's laughter… his tiny footsteps running across this courtyard. My family… will return."

And for the first time in many years, the silence in the house didn't feel empty. It felt expectant—as if the earth holding its breath before the rain.

Chapter 9

Cutting through the rocks

On the sacred morning of Ganeshotsav, the house brimmed with movement, fragrance, and quiet excitement. The rhythmic rustling of banana leaves, the aroma of steaming modaks, and the soft clang of utensils created a festival symphony. Savitri moved through the rooms like a steady flame—decorating, cooking, preparing the Prasad with reverence and motherly love.

By afternoon, the courtyard was adorned with garlands, rangoli, and devotion. The Ganapati puja began with Savitri leading the rituals, her voice trembling with chants that seemed to rise from the deepest corners of her heart. One by one, Nilkanth's students gathered—humble, awed, and silently grateful to be a part of something beyond themselves. As they joined hands for the aarti, the flame reflected in their eyes—full of dreams, burdens, and a quiet, burning hope.

Once the aarti ended and prasad was served, the students dispersed, each carrying with them a piece of peace.

But for Nilkanth and his four boys, the true purpose of the day was only just beginning.

Together, with Savitri joining in, they walked towards the site beside the courtyard—the dry old well that once breathed life into the village. There, they lay before Bappa not just flowers and incense, but maps, tools, and blueprints—every line and angle drawn with sweats and vision. With reverent hands, they offered puja to the very instruments that would carve hope from stone—compasses, chisels ropes, spades, and leveling rods.

The air grew still as Savitri and Nilkanth stood side by side, folding their hands before the ancient earth and the silent deity.

"Bappa," they whispered in unison, "no matter what comes, we will not falter. This village must be blessed before your next arrival. Let our hands be steady, our faith unshaken. Give us strength to carry this burden with love."

In a moment that felt both sacred and fierce, Nilkanth lifted the pickaxe and brought it down at the edge of the long-silent well—its sharp clang against stone echoing like a temple bell through the still air.

And then, Savitri stepped forward. Holding a shreephal (coconut) in her hands, her eyes closed in surrender, she smashed it against the stone with a cry in her heart—not of fear, but of offering. Of surrender. Of will.

The pieces scattered across the dry soil.

A beginning was born.

All six of them stood silent, eyes moist, hearts full. Not one of them would turn back now.

That evening, the project began—not with fanfare, but with hands and resolve. All five of them—Nilkanth, Suresh, Mohan, Prakash, and Pankaj—gathered at the edge of the old, forgotten well. Together, they started clearing the area. The overgrown grass, the thorny acacia bushes, the entangled roots and debris—each handful thrown aside was a step closer to a dream long buried under layers of neglect.

With each weed uprooted, they felt like they were also clearing out years of despair and drought.

By nightfall, the land lay bare—clean, sacred, and waiting.

Under the dim glow of the lantern, they sat and drew up a detailed shift plan, ensuring that digging would continue without pause while allowing each of them to rest and recover. Nilkanth, true to his silent endurance, chose the night hours for himself. "The stars," he had said with a wry smile, "keep better company for old men." But it was more than that. The land belonged to him, and so did the burden. He wanted to be the last one holding the chisel each night, even if no one else saw. And so, day and night merged.

Days passed. Then weeks. Then months. Through cold mornings and silent winter midnights, the sound of metal striking stone became their secret rhythm. As the shaft went through a certain angle the earth responded slowly, yielding layer after stubborn layer. And as the well deepened, something incredible took shape—a staircase, cut by hand, gently slanted downwards shaft like a breaking through the several layers of rocks and then reached the clay of hope. It was not just practical—it was graceful, like a sculpture carved inside the earth itself. Although as Nilkanth studied the land there was many more layers of black rocks to reach the water base.

But no miracle can remain hidden for long.

As the nights grew colder, the rhythmic clang of hammer and chisel began to travel—echoing through the stillness of the village. The sounds were faint at first, like whispers of the past waking up. But the nearest neighbors, roused from sleep, started to murmur. "What's happening at the Jadhav house?" "Why is there digging at midnight?" "Is it for a temple? A tunnel? Something else?" The rumors began to brew.

But Savitri, with her calm gaze and quick wit, handled every question like a seasoned diplomat. Over cups of chai and temple visits, she crafted stories that veiled the truth yet satisfied curiosity. Nilkanth, when asked, would smile vaguely and talk about an "art experiment" or a "Sculpture designing."

What they hid was not out of fear—but faith that the truth would be revealed only when the time was ripe.

And until then, their labor continued—stone by stone, night by night, and heartbeat by heartbeat.

But even the most promising days are often shadowed by looming hardships.

Nilkanth and his four loyal students — Suresh, Mohan, Prashant, and Pankaj — had tirelessly carved their way downward through layers of stone, etching a shaft into the belly of the earth angular path getting deep inside. Their steady descent had finally reached the clay zone — damp, unstable, and perilous. This was the most treacherous layer; the weight of loose clay and buried boulders could collapse at any moment, threatening to entomb anyone below.

Thankfully, Prashant had meticulously installed LED lights every 5 to 10 meters, illuminating the shaft like a glowing spine deep into the ground. Still, each descent required them to tie strong nylon ropes around their waists, fastened to a fixed iron pillar above — their only lifeline in case of an accident.

But the cold season was creeping in. And within that depth, the damp chill was even harsher than the air above. The men labored through the night, the moisture settling on their skin, chilling their breath, weighing down their strength.

Nilkanth, weathered but stubborn, took on more than his share of the midnight shifts. Then one morning, his breath grew heavy — a deep, hacking cough tearing through his chest. Savitri found him collapsed near the well's rim, burning with fever and gasping for air.

Panic seized her heart.

With the help of the boys, they rushed him to the village government hospital. The doctors, alarmed, referred him immediately to Ratnagiri. Test results came back grim: severe lung congestion, likely pneumonia. At his age, the risk was high. They admitted him straight into the ICU.

Savitri stood frozen outside the ward, clutching the hospital railings as tears silently rolled down her face. But Nilkanth, even through an oxygen mask, had one firm command:

"Do not call Vinayak."

So, without a second thought, Savitri unclasped her gold chain — the one Nilkanth had given her on their first Ganesh Chaturthi as a married couple — and sold it to pay the hospital bills.

Back in the village, Nilkanth's students made a silent vow:

"We will not stop. We will dig, shift by shift, until Sir returns. No delays."

They worked with double the spirit and twice the care, knowing every blow of their pickaxes was a prayer for his recovery.

Days crawled by. A week passed. Nilkanth's fever lingered, and doctors confirmed traces of pneumonia. Though treatable, his age made the road ahead uncertain. Meanwhile, Savitri — running endlessly between hospital wards and village needs — began to weaken herself, her body surrendering to fatigue. Yet she never once informed Vinayak or Jayashree. She bore the storm alone, trusting Bappa and her boys.

At last, on the eighth morning, the doctors shifted Nilkanth to the general ward. His fever had lowered his breathing calmer. It was a flicker of hope — just enough to lift Savitri's spirit.

And that very morning, as the doctor left the ward, Prashant arrived breathless, a wild gleam in his eyes.

He peeked in and saw Nilkanth asleep, frail and pale, and hurried instead to Savitri who sat outside, her hands wrapped around a lukewarm cup of tea.

"Madam!" he whispered, breathless, "May I wake Sir? I have something important — something that might help him heal faster!"

Savitri looked up, startled. "Is everything alright? Are you boys' safe?"

"Yes, yes!" Prashant nodded quickly, barely containing himself. "It's actually good news, Madam. Very good news. I truly believe it will bring him back to health!"

A faint light flickered in her tired eyes. "Tell me… have you found a sign? A trace of water?"

Prashant's eyes widened with joy. "Yes, exactly! Now we were close to 40 meters down. We've gone through stone, clay, and now we've begun chiseling into the dense black rock. And last night — just last night — as we struck the black rock, a fine spray of water burst from the cracks! It wasn't much, but it sprayed, Madam! Like the earth exhaled for the first time in decades!"

Savitri dropped her paper cup of tea in the dustbin. Her hands flew to her mouth, tears rushing down her cheeks before she could speak. "Oh Bappa… you've heard us at last."

Prashant gently added, "Please, let me tell him. I know our Sir needs this more than any medicine. These words will be like Sanjeevani for him."

Still trembling, Savitri held his hand and smiled through her tears.

"Yes, beta! Please… go. Go wake him. Tell him the earth has whispered back."

Savitri quietly stepped into the hospital room, her tired feet moving gently across the cold floor. She sat beside Nilkanth's bed and placed her hand softly on his forehead. The warmth lingered — the nurse had said it was still around 100°F that morning. Her fingers trembled as they brushed back his greying hair, now damp with sweat.

Slowly, Nilkanth stirred, his eyelids fluttering open. His voice, dry and cracking from sleep and illness, barely formed words:

"Savitri... did you have tea? Something to eat? I must've dozed off again. Is there any word from the boys? How are they managing?"

A short pause. Then, his brow creased with worry.

"They mustn't give up. I'll be back with them soon… But—why are your eyes moist? Did the doctor… show you something again? Something worse?"

Savitri swallowed her tears and forced a fragile smile. She tilted her head, directing his eyes to the corner of the room — where Prashant stood quietly, holding a tiny bottle clutched close to his chest.

Nilkanth turned his gaze and blinked.

"Prashant beta! What are you doing here? You must've worked all night! Why didn't you rest, son?"

Even through his pain, Nilkanth's first thought was for the boy's well-being.

Prashant couldn't hold back anymore. His eyes brimmed, and a sob escaped him — not of sorrow, but of overwhelming joy. He rushed to the bedside, took Nilkanth's frail hands in both of his own, and cried out:

"Sir! We found it! We found water! It sprayed out through the black rocks last night — just a trickle, but it was real! Real water, Sir! I've brought some with me, in this bottle... for you."

Nilkanth jolted upright as though new life surged through him.

"You're serious? Prashant! This… this is from our land? From the womb of this stubborn, rocky village?"

His voice cracked with disbelief, eyes glistening with pride and awe.

"Bappa heard us... He heard us... I knew it! I knew this land still had a heart left!"

He tried to sit up, almost springing from the bed.

"I must go back today — right now! We need to be careful now. The rocks can become unstable with that water pressure. The shaft must be secured—this is the most delicate part!"

But before he could swing his legs off the bed, Savitri rushed to his side and gripped his arm firmly.

"No, Nilkanth! No way! You are not going anywhere unless the doctor allows it. Don't act like a stubborn child now."

Her voice trembled, laced with both love and fear.

"Yes, the boys will wait. They will all wait. But you… you will get well first. Promise me that."

Nilkanth looked at her, eyes burning with resolve.

"But Savitri, I'm fine now. Look at me! I'll take my medicines properly — I swear. But I have to be there. This isn't just a well anymore. It's a promise. A dream. A prayer buried in every layer of soil we touched."

He turned to Prashant with urgency, clutching his hand.

"Beta, please… speak to the doctors. See if they'll allow me to leave today, even if for a while. I need to see it — with my own eyes."

Prashant looked at both of them — his Sir, blazing with unstoppable spirit despite the weakness in his body, and Madam, holding back her pain to protect the man she loved more than life itself. He felt torn but inspired.

With a soft nod, he said:

"Sir, I will talk to the doctors. But only if you promise to rest first. No more excitement, no more stress. We will all wait for you, just as you've waited for the water. That's a promise."

Savitri glanced at the little bottle in Prashant's hand — a humble vial holding a miracle — and whispered through her tears:

"Bappa has answered. Now let Him heal what He has begun to bless."

The boys had halted the digging. With the first sign of water confirmed, they now turned their attention to securing the shaft. Together, they began plastering the internal walls with a sticky, reddish-brown soil — a mix known to hold firm and endure pressure. They knew it wasn't just about finding water anymore; the space had to be safe, welcoming. Something livable, almost sacred. The staircase they had carved through the shaft cutting stone now curved gently into the earth, waiting to carry the villagers down to the miracle that slept beneath their feet.

Meanwhile, Nilkanth's health began to improve. The fever slowly waned. His breathing grew easier. Each day brought a little more color back to his worn face, and Savitri, though exhausted, breathed easier too.

Word had begun to trickle through the village. Curious neighbors came to visit him at the hospital, some with fruits or flowers, and others just with folded hands and quiet prayers. Many asked about his sculpture work — the same story Savitri had carefully planted in case anyone grew suspicious of the digging. Nilkanth, weak but determined, would smile and say:

"The work is nearly done. Soon I'll show you all myself."

Some pushed further, asking to see the creation. But neither Nilkanth nor Savitri budged.

"Patience," he would reply, with a flicker in his eyes,

"Art reveals itself only when it's ready."

No one — not even the most observant neighbors — could guess the truth hidden behind the tarpaulin tent stretched over the backyard of Jadhav's quiet house. Beneath that tent, revolution took root in soil and sweat.

Five days passed. On the sixth morning, the doctor walked into Nilkanth's room, smiling.

"All vitals look good. You're fit to go home."

The news filled Nilkanth with joy. He almost leapt from the bed, eager to return to his boys, to the unfinished well that called to him like a child calling its father.

But that joy was short-lived.

Savitri's phone rang.

It was Jayashree.

Her voice, gentle and shaking, carried more weight than any fever could.

She had found out.

Jayashree's cousin, Dr. Kiran, happened to be working in the same hospital. Until now, she hadn't connected the dots. But the night before, during a casual call, Jayashree had mentioned Sir. That's when the truth slipped out — Nilkanth had been in ICU for nearly two weeks.

Now, Jayashree and Vinayak were already packing, ready to board the next bus.

The storm broke when Nilkanth grabbed Savitri's phone and called his son.

It was the first time he had spoken directly to Vinayak in years.

His voice, though aged and hoarse, cracked like thunder.

"Vinayak," he said, "swear to me — you both will not come. I'm fine. I've been discharged. Your mother and my students are enough for me. There's no need to waste your time, money, or leave your office."

There was silence on the other end, but Nilkanth didn't pause.

"Swear on me that you'll stay where you are. When the time comes — and it will come — I'll call you myself. Until then, stay back. That is my last word."

He hung up.

At the other end, Vinayak stood frozen, the bag half-packed, Jayashree beside him with her hands still folded around the clothes. Their hearts trembled — not from anger, but from helplessness. For the first time, they'd heard not just distance, but pain, in Baba's voice.

Jayashree couldn't stop herself. She dialed again — this time, Savitri.

Her voice cracked as she pleaded:

"Hello… Aai? Why won't you both let us come? Please don't shut us out. We didn't know Baba was in the hospital neither you informed us. I spoke to my cousin Kiran last night — she only realized yesterday he's our Baba . Please, Aai… let us come. Just once. Let us hold your hands. Let us say sorry... for not being there."

Savitri's throat burned. She pressed her hand to her chest, trying to still the ache. Her eyes welled up but her voice stayed steady — heavy, but resolute.

"Beti," she said softly, "I can't go against his will. You heard him. He's not ready yet. But listen to me carefully — we will see you soon. You, Vinayak, and little Advait. All of us, together."

A pause.

"We are fine… truly. So take care of yourselves until then. That's all we ask."

And before Jayashree could respond, Savitri ended the call — gently, but firmly.

She placed the phone down, wiped her tears, and turned to the corridor where Nilkanth waited near the parapet of a balcony, staring silently at the morning sun.

Neither spoke.

But in that silence, a thousand unsaid words passed between them — of love, of regret, of hope and above all, of unfinished healing of their aching heart for their beloved family.

As the cab rolled to a stop outside his home, Nilkanth opened the door before the engine could quiet. He handed the driver the fare with trembling fingers — not from weakness, but anticipation. The midday sun blazed over the hills, but Nilkanth's eyes searched only one thing — the tarp-covered well behind his house.

He walked briskly, heart pounding with a strange blend of relief and urgency. The tarpaulin flapped gently in the breeze like a curtain pulled back on a stage. He stepped through, and there it stood — the well.

The shaft was no longer just a shaft within the ground but the inner walls were now coated with a thick, smooth layer of earth plaster. It looked firm, secure — as if it had always belonged there.

Inside, he saw Suresh and Mohan, sleeves rolled up, their hands caked in sticky clay as they worked with practiced rhythm.

"Sir!" Suresh called out, surprised, his face breaking into a smile. "You should've called us! We would have picked you up."

Nilkanth waved a hand, brushing the concern aside. "I had to see it first... before anything else."

Without another word, he moved to the stairs and began his slow descent, one hand on the wall for support. His breath deepened as he sank farther into the cool, damp belly of the earth. Each step felt like a return — not just to a place, but to a purpose.

When he reached the bottom, his eyes scanned the black rock where Prashant had claimed water had appeared.

And there it was.

A narrow slit in the stone pulsed softly with a thin spray of glistening water, like veins in rock breathing life again. The droplets struck the wall opposite and trickled down the sides of the chamber, soaking the soil in gentle patterns.

Nilkanth crouched and touched it. Cold. Fresh. Alive.

His heart swelled — not just with triumph, but caution. He examined the surrounding area. The black rock layer was thinner here, brittle in places. Any further digging without reinforcement could be dangerous.

He stood and turned to the boys.

"Suresh, Mohan — you've done excellent work," he said, voice steady with pride. "But listen to me — leave it for now. Go home. Rest."

He paused. "By evening, we'll all gather. We must rethink our next steps — no haste, no risk. The water is here… but if we go deeper, it must be safe. This isn't just about digging anymore. It's about responsibility."

The boys nodded, understanding the weight in his voice. They climbed out together, but Nilkanth lingered for a few moments longer, staring at the trickle from the rock.

He whispered, more to the well than to himself —

"Bappa… your blessings have begun to flow. Now guide our hands… steady our hearts."

Then, slowly, with a faint smile on his lips and resolve burning in his chest, he climbed back toward the light.

The sun dipped behind the western hills, casting a golden hue across the verandah. The day's heat mellowed into a soft breeze, carrying with it the smell of wet earth and warm tea. A steel kettle sat on the low wooden table beside a tray of cups, still steaming. The four young men—Suresh, Mohan, Prashant, and Pankaj—sat cross-legged on mats laid out on the ground. Nilkanth joined them, leaning on a cane, while Savitri sat nearby in her old cane chair, her sari draped loosely over her shoulders, eyes calm yet vigilant.

Nilkanth, sat with a file of sketches and diagrams spread across his lap. The others waited, watching him flip through the pages. The quiet was broken only by the occasional clink of a cup or the rustle of paper.

Nilkanth finally looked up and said, his tone serious, "There are two concerns we need to address—urgently."

Everyone leaned in, the stillness sharpening.

He tapped on a detailed cross-section Prashant had drawn. "First—the black rock layer. It's solid, yes. But the moment moisture seeps into the joints from the underlying clay, its structural integrity can weaken. If we continue digging without reinforcing the walls further, a collapse is possible—especially when water pressure builds."

Nilkanth nodded gravely. "I saw it today. The rock has already started to sweat. This is no longer a simple dig." He continued, "Second—there's the matter of the excavated material. We've removed tons of rock and clay over the last ten months. At first, it was manageable, but now the pile is huge. Some villagers have started asking questions. A few have even guessed something unusual is going on. I've been telling them it's all for the stone sculpture project, but..."

He glanced at Savitri. She sipped her tea slowly and said, "The excuse won't hold much longer. They're beginning to wonder how one idol could require such volume."

Pankaj muttered, "And if they start poking around the tarp…"

Suresh added, "We've kept them away so far, but curiosity is growing. A few kids even tried sneaking in last week. Mohan caught them just in time before they could lift the tarpaulin cover."

Nilkanth drew a slow breath. "Then we must act quickly. Complete the lower lining of the shaft, seal the layers with binding clay, and reinforce the walls before we go any further. No more digging until we're sure it's safe."

Prashant said thoughtfully, "We can also start moving the excess clay and rocks to the old dry riverbed beyond the east slope by arranging an EV carrier from tonight. It's distant enough, and if we carry loads at night in small quantities, no one will notice."

Mohan nodded. "I'll handle the logistics. I have a friend of mine who have a EV carrier to make the transfer easier. We can call him for dinner if Madam allow and give him some few hundred to complete the same work. I will be with him "

Nilkanth leaned back, folding the papers. "Good. But let's also prepare for one more thing—if the villagers press harder, we may have to show them something. May be a stone sculpture which we have at workshop we can bring that here."

The tea cooled slowly as the sun finally vanished behind the banyan tree. A silence settled over the group again, but this time, it was not of fear or doubt—it was of determination.

Savitri, watching each of them, felt a deep stirring in her chest. These boys had become more than disciples. They were torchbearers of a forgotten promise.

She whispered, almost inaudibly—

"Bappa... the roots have found water. Now let the tree rise."

That night, under the veil of darkness and the soft glow of lanterns, the movement of stone and clay debris began. From behind the house, the boys quietly hauled load after load toward the back trail, dumping them into the unused ravine near the eastern slope. The rhythmic thud of soil and the rumble of the wheelbarrow wheels continued well past midnight. By the time the first birds chirped their dawn song, the ground behind the Jadhav home stood clear again.

Nilkanth watched from a distance, leaning against a pillar. A quiet sense of relief unfurled within him. The mounting weight of worry, suspicion, and clutter had finally begun to lift.

The following afternoon, as the sun poured in through the open windows and the smell of lemon grass tea filled the air, Nilkanth called the boys together. They gathered under the shade of the banyan, notebooks and bottles of water in hand.

"I've been thinking," Nilkanth said, his eyes gleaming with a new spark. "We need better support inside the shaft as we go deeper. The clay joints near the black rock are soft, and with water already seeping through, we can't risk a collapse."

He looked around at the curious faces. "What if," he continued, "we use old, discarded fishing boats as forms—forma—to reinforce the joints? We'll stabilize them using rods and timber logs. The curvature of the hulls could cradle the inner walls and absorb the pressure."

The boys blinked, stunned for a moment.

Then Suresh exclaimed, "Sir! That's brilliant. It'll act like a mold and barrier at once."

Encouraged, Nilkanth added, "If we install them in segments, adjusting the size to the narrowing shaft, it might just give us the reinforcement we need."

Prashant, who had been scribbling something rapidly in his notebook, suddenly looked up, his eyes bright. "Sir! I was researching last night. There's a tool—an electric hand breaker which is much more efficient than a pickaxe or crowbar. It breaks rock without the high-impact vibration, so the surrounding structure remains more stable. We can chip away at the black rock precisely and gradually taper the base till we reach the ground water level."

Nilkanth's face lit up, pride warming his chest like a fire. He patted Prashant's shoulder. "That's thinking like an engineer, beta. I'm proud of you. We'll find a way to get that machine."

Energized, he stood up and turned to Suresh. "Didn't you once say your uncle knows someone who rebuilds boats?"

"Yes, Sir! Altaf Chacha. He's a master carpenter and boat maker. He might still have hulls he discarded from his last repair."

"Then let's not waste time. Take me to him," Nilkanth said, already reaching for his slippers.

Meanwhile, Pankaj was already tapping his phone, speaking to someone in a hushed voice. When he ended the call, he grinned. "Sir, my elder brother knows a contractor. They have a hand breaker—they rent it out for demolitions and trenching. I'll go and confirm the rental terms. I think we can get it by next week."

Nilkanth looked around at the boys, each of them, so different, so full of ideas and initiative. They weren't just helping—they were building something sacred, together.

The old sculptor smiled his voice soft but steady.

"Now it's not just me. It's us. This well isn't being carved out of stone. It's being carved out of faith."

Savitri, watching from the kitchen door, wiped her hands on her sari and stood still for a moment—her eyes misty, her heart full.

By the following afternoon, the ground behind the Jadhav home buzzed with renewed energy. The hand breaker arrived on a bullock cart, wrapped in tarpaulin and tied down with coarse ropes. Pankaj, panting and dust-covered, leapt off and proudly announced, "It's here! And I've learned how to use it from dada. We're good to go."

Just an hour earlier, Suresh had returned with three discarded boats—weather-worn, cracked, and smelling faintly of sea salt and engine grease. Altaf Chacha, the boatmaker, had burst into laughter when Suresh explained what they planned to do with them.

"Arrey beta, are you designing a Noah's ark?" he had teased, while handing them over free of cost. "But if it's you, I know even broken boats will float."

Suresh, undeterred, smiled and replied, "They'll hold more than water, Chacha. They'll hold faith."

The team split into two. Mohan, Pankaj, and Nilkanth set up a shaded workspace near the well, laying the boats on their sides and marking out segments. The soft thwack-thwack of saws and the sharp ring of chisels soon filled the air as they shaped the curved hulls into arched supports that could nestle into the shaft walls like ribs in a tunnel.

At the well's mouth, Suresh and Prashant began the descent. Harnessed securely, they lowered the breaker into the shaft. Suresh, with his solid frame and practiced grip, took to the machine naturally. It shuddered softly in his hands—its low-vibration mechanism eating into the black rock without sending dangerous tremors through the shaft.

The rock cracked in clean shards, dust rising like incense. Between every shift, they paused for rest—sipping chaas, wiping sweat, sharing jokes. But the tempo never dropped.

Each chisel, each broken slab, each section of curved boat wood lifted down into the dark was a quiet testimony to their stubborn will.

Above, Savitri watched from the porch, her hands folded in silent prayer. Below, the boys worked not just as students, but as sons. And Nilkanth—his eyes tracking each stroke, each movement—felt something he hadn't felt in years.

Not just hope, but the beginning of legacy.

As the days passed and the clink of stone against steel became a familiar echo in the air, the scent of festivity slowly wafted through the village lanes—Shimgotsav had arrived.

Bright colors returned to the sleepy settlement. Children ran about with pichkaris, women sang age-old ovi, and the men prepared the communal fire for the Holika Dahan. Amidst this, Nilkanth surprised his students with a quiet announcement: "This year, we'll celebrate Shimgotsav right here—at the workshop."

Savitri, heart swelling with pride and quiet emotion, busied herself in the kitchen. She made karanji, chakli, and her special coconut laddoos, their aroma spreading across the courtyard like a whisper of old warmth. One by one, the boys arrived—each bearing tiffins and small steel containers with home-cooked dishes from their mothers: spicy batatyachi bhaaji, puran poli, modak, and tangy sol kadhi. The little space behind the house turned into a celebration of taste, laughter, and shared struggle.

As the group sat together on straw mats under the tarpaulin sky, their hands greasy with ghee and laughter echoing around the plastered shaft, Savitri paused for a moment. She looked at them—Nilkanth, thinner but more alive than ever; Suresh, breaking into a spontaneous folk song; Mohan with his habitual, thoughtful grin; Pankaj cracking jokes; Prashant talking animatedly about water-pressure mapping.

Her eyes moistened. It had almost been a year.

A year of stubborn digging through stone and silence. A year of scraped palms, midnight echoes of metal on rock, and whispered prayers at dawn. A year of hiding truths from neighbors, and dreams from even their own family. But now—now something was shifting.

It wasn't just a celebration of Shimgotsav. It was a thanksgiving for the harvest of their own endurance. A festival of a dream that had roots now—deep and irreversible.

And somewhere beneath their feet, beyond the reach of prayer or planning, the water was stirring too.

After Shimgotsav, the team returned to the well with renewed fire in their hearts. The festival had not just marked a celebration—it had reignited a collective vow: they would finish the work before the cruel summer arrived to parch the village once more. Nilkanth, wiser from months of toil and illness, designed a work cycle with equal parts labour and rest. The shaft was nearly complete, its walls reinforced and narrowing like the neck of an hourglass—time was slipping, but they would not let it run dry.

Then, one dawn, it happened.

A tremor deep below the surface. A gasp of earth long strangled. And a roar.

Suresh shouted.

A thunderous gush of water had blasted through the black rock with such force, it threw him backwards—breaker and all—out of the shaft and onto the slope, as if the mountain itself had finally surrendered. Startled but unhurt, drenched and wide-eyed, he sat blinking under the sky, water splashing around him like some divine welcome.

Prashant screamed, his voice cracking with disbelief, "Sir! Sir! Wake up! It's happened—we've struck it! The water—it's alive, it threw us out! It's sweet, it's wild!"

Nilkanth, half asleep after a long night shift, jolted up. Savitri sat up too, confused by the frenzy. But before she could ask, he had already flung on a T-shirt, still in his half-pants, and bolted barefoot across the courtyard.

He reached the shaft to find Suresh emerging—mud-caked, triumphant, carrying the breaker in one hand like a soldier returning from war. His eyes gleamed.

Nilkanth didn't wait. He ran forward and wrapped him in a fierce embrace.

"You did it, my boy," he whispered hoarsely. "You've made the mountain bleed life."

Prashant joined them, breathless and grinning, and they both fell at Nilkanth's feet. Tears glistened in the corners of the old man's eyes. He steadied himself and said, voice trembling yet firm,

"Now… we seal this miracle. Suresh, drop the breaker—it's done its duty. Let's fix the pipes."

Two large concrete pipes lay nearby, brought days earlier in anticipation. The boys rolled the first using wooden logs, maneuvering it into the shaft. They waded through the rising water, the flow fierce and clean as a newborn spring. Reaching the outlet point, they heaved the pipe into position, muscles straining, heartbeats racing. The moment it aligned, the gushing water funneled through it with roaring clarity.

Suresh leapt forward, laying the bricks and mortar to seal the pipe. Prashant rushed out for more supplies. Water continued to pour—now tamed, but not yet tapped.

Soon, Mohan and Pankaj arrived, bringing the second pipe. It was fitted with a collar joint, perfectly locking in the flow and lifting it above the surface. With the shaft stabilized and the water pressure now channeled, they needed just one final element: a heavy-duty pressure pump to raise the water and supply the village.

Exhausted, soaked, yet electrified, the boys cleaned themselves up and sat around Nilkanth in the courtyard, the early morning sun glowing on their proud, muddy faces.

Nilkanth looked at them all—his boys, his disciples—and said softly,

"Now, it's time to call the BDO. We need that pump. The battle is half-won—but the revolution begins now."

The next morning, Nilkanth approached BDO Ghanshyam Dongre to request a pump. Known for his corruption, Dongre scoffed at the idea. "You're an idol-maker, not an engineer. Running a government isn't child's play!" he sneered, flinging the application in Nilkanth's face. "Don't waste my time—and don't expect anything without a generous under-the-table offer." His words dripped with arrogance. Suresh clenched his jaw in rage, while Prashant, calm and cunning, secretly recorded the entire exchange from his shirt pocket. Unknowingly, Ghanshyam sealed his own downfall—his pride and corruption exposed by the very people he tried to belittle.

After stepping out of the BDO's office, Suresh fumed his voice thick with anger. "This Ghanshyam was a beggar once—now just because he's a BDO, he thinks he owns the village! He should've rushed to see the well, but instead—"

Nilkanth gently placed a hand on his shoulder and said with a calm smile, "Easy, my child. Every rise is followed by a fall. I have contact details of a geological surveyor and a scientist—Madam Lalitha from Suratkal. Let me reach out to them. Perhaps they can help."

Just then, Prashant came running with a packet of snacks. "Sir! I recorded the entire conversation with Ghanshyam. His own words will come back to haunt him."

Nilkanth chuckled softly. "Ah, youth! It's natural for you to react. But remember—resistance often leads to revelation. I actually thank Ghanshyam in my heart. One day, you'll understand why... and you'll remember these very words."

As soon as they reached the well site, Nilkanth called Madam Lalitha, who had earlier asked him to keep her updated on the water situation in the village—especially since he had taken the initiative to tackle the scarcity. The call barely rang once before she picked up.

"Hello, Madam Lalitha?" he greeted.

"Nilkanthji! I'm so glad to hear from you. I was beginning to wonder why there had been no updates, especially with summer already at our doorstep," she said warmly.

Nilkanth replied with a humble smile, "Forgive me, Madam. My team and I have been working tirelessly, digging a well by hand. And... we did it. We've struck water. Now, we need your help."

Lalitha gasped with joy. "What! You mean you've found groundwater? That's incredible! Please, tell me everything. Can you show me on a video call, if the network allows?"

With moist eyes and a cracking voice, Nilkanth responded, "Yes, Madam. My team will show you the well live. I think the network should hold."

As the video call connected, the camera panned down the shaft, where Prashant had climbed to the base and pointed it toward the fitted pipeline. Despite occasional glitches, Lalitha could grasp the scale of their achievement.

"This is amazing!" she exclaimed. "Now tell me, Nilkanthji—what exactly do you need from us?"

With tears welling up, Nilkanth replied, "For the past year, we've dug this shaft because, as you said, machines couldn't be brought here. Today, we've reached water—but we want every thirsty villager to benefit from it. We need government support to install pressure pumps and distribute this water to every home."

Lalitha smiled warmly. "Don't worry, Nilkanthji. By tomorrow, your efforts will be acknowledged. I'll do everything I can. We're coming to your village to witness this miracle ourselves."

As the call ended—on speaker for all to hear—everyone burst into cheers of joy. Overwhelmed with emotion, Nilkanth rushed inside to share the news with Savitri, his voice trembling with happiness. Meanwhile, the four boys got back to work, giving the well shaft its final finishing touches. They carefully sealed the pipe outlet with a disposable bottle and cloth to prevent even a single drop of the precious water from going to waste.

The next morning marked a true dawn—not just for Nilkanth and his four boys, but for the entire village. They were on the verge of witnessing something that had once seemed impossible.

After brushing his teeth and inspecting the well shaft as usual, Nilkanth returned to the living room with his tea and newspaper. Just then, the sound of a cab halting outside caught his attention. He rushed to the window, and before he could speak, Savitri called out with a teasing laugh, "At least change out of that lungi and T-shirt! No one's going to take you seriously dressed like that!"

Peering out, Nilkanth whispered with quiet urgency, "It's Madam Lalitha—with her team. Please go welcome her. I'll be right there."

He hurried inside, quickly changed into a formal shirt and trousers, and stepped out with folded hands, his heart pounding with anticipation. Lalitha smiled warmly as she stepped out of the car and said, "Ah, Nilkanthji! We're eager to witness the miracle. Please, take us to the site right away."

As they approached the tarpaulin-covered site, Lalitha and her team were taken aback by the sheer scale and care of the arrangements. Nilkanth quietly called for all four boys to join, knowing the scientists might suggest critical improvements before finalizing the shaft.

Descending the staircase—illuminated by LED lights placed at thoughtful intervals—Lalitha and her team stepped carefully along the smooth, hand-carved path cut through stone and clay. The precision was undeniable. Pathways had been etched to accommodate pipelines and future maintenance, and every step bore testimony to a year's worth of silent, relentless labor.

When they reached the clay-layered zone—reinforced ingeniously with arched supports made from discarded boats—the engineers were left speechless. What would normally cost lakhs in professional excavation had been executed with local intelligence, salvaged materials, and pure willpower.

By the time they reached the black rock stratum deep within the shaft, they spotted the outlet pipe—its mouth plugged with a cloth-stuffed bottle. Nilkanth turned to the group and gently said, "Please stand back." He knelt beside the pipe, whispering a prayer to Bappa, his heart pounding with hope—for the boys, for the village, for the water that had remained just out of reach for decades.

With steady hands, he untied the cloth. The moment he pulled the bottle free, a powerful jet of water erupted, spraying across the shaft floor and soaking their feet. It was as if the earth itself had opened its arms to welcome them.

For a second, no one moved. Then came the cheers—Lalitha clapped with tearful wonder, the engineers stood stunned, and the four boys shouted with unrestrained joy. The miracle was no longer a dream. It had come alive, rushing forth from the depths, baptized by toil and hope.

Lalitha, overwhelmed with emotion, called Nilkanth over, grasped his hand firmly, and said with a wide, heartfelt smile, "Nilkanthji, this is both unbelievable and deeply commendable. What you and your boys have achieved is nothing short of a miracle."

She paused for a moment, still holding his hand, then added with conviction, "I'll speak to the ministers immediately and ensure that arrangements are made to pump this water to every household in the village. In the meantime, our team of engineers will begin surveying the area to design an effective pipeline distribution network."

Then, with eyes full of admiration, she said, "You've brought the water to the surface. Now let me take over from here, to fulfill your dream of quenching the thirst of every home in this village."

As Lalitha emerged from the well shaft, she found a large crowd of villagers gathered near the tent, curious and anxious to know the outcome. But before anyone could ask, she raised her voice and declared with pride,

"You all must be grateful to Nilkanthji. The man who once sculpted idols for your prayers has now sculpted a miracle beneath your feet. With the help of these four brilliant boys, he has carved a path to water—your most precious need. This shaft is your lifeline, born from their sweat, patience, and determination."

A wave of awe swept through the crowd. In a spontaneous burst of emotion, the villagers erupted into applause. Cheering loudly, they lifted Nilkanth and the four boys—Suresh, Mohan, Prashant, and Pankaj—onto their shoulders, chanting:

"Hail to our beloved Nilkanth, Suresh, Mohan, Prashant, and Pankaj!"

From a quiet corner of the courtyard, Savitri watched through tear-filled eyes. She clasped her hands in prayer and whispered her thanks to Bappa. A village long parched of joy now overflowed—not just with water, but with tears of gratitude and celebration.

Chapter 10

The Home coming

Nilkanth folded his hands in gratitude to the villagers, then gently took Savitri's hand and led her to Madam Lalitha. His voice trembled with emotion as he said,

"Madam, if it weren't for my better half, my wife Savitri, I wouldn't be standing here today. During the hardest days, when I was hospitalized with pneumonia, it was she—and my four young warriors—who stood by me. She is my anchor, my strength, my silent inspiration."

Savitri lowered her gaze, tears flowing freely down her cheeks. Lalitha stepped forward and embraced her warmly, saying,

"There's no doubt, Nilkanthji draws his courage and resolve from you. Behind every great man stands a woman like you."

She smiled, then added with a light chuckle,

"Now come, let's sit for some tea. I have many calls to make—and even more good news to share."

Lalitha turned to the gathered villagers and announced,

"Now that Nilkanthji and all of you are about to make headlines, I'm sure we'll meet again—many times—for even greater celebrations. Thank you for your patience, your faith, and your unity."

With that, she and her team returned to Nilkanth's house to begin discussing the next steps for village-wide water distribution. Meanwhile, Savitri had already laid out tea and snacks, serving everyone with quiet joy.

With a steaming cup of tea in one hand, Lalitha began dialing key officials—starting with the District Magistrate, then the Chief Secretaries of the state. She paused mid-call and turned to Nilkanth, asking,

"Nilkanthji, have you informed the BDO yet?"

Before he could respond, Prashant quickly stepped forward and said,

"Madam, we did go to meet him. But you need to see what actually happened."

Nilkanth's face darkened slightly, and he scolded,

"Prashant, no—please, don't trouble Madam with this."

But the video had already started playing from Prashant's phone. Lalitha's expression shifted to one of concern and quiet fury. She raised a hand and said firmly,

"Prashant, send me that video immediately."

Nilkanth wasn't entirely pleased with Prashant's impulsive action, but his four young warriors couldn't hide their satisfaction. Deep down, they felt justice would finally be served—that Ghanshyam would face consequences for insulting their beloved mentor.

Not long after, the pressure pump arrived at the site, dispatched under orders from the SDM following Lalitha's strong recommendation. Engineers, along with a team of plumbers and electricians, assembled swiftly. The pipeline network began to take shape with remarkable speed. That evening, Lalitha retired to the village guesthouse, accompanied by her colleagues from the Geological Survey team—among them, Madam Suman and Siddharth Sir, whom Nilkanth had met nearly a decade ago in 2016. It was they who had once suggested the possibility of groundwater beneath that very land.

The entire day unfolded like a dream, so surreal that Nilkanth, his team, and even Savitri could barely absorb its joy and momentum.

Later that night, after dinner, Nilkanth and Savitri stepped outside to witness the ongoing pipeline work. Standing under the quiet sky, lights flickering across the dusty road, he whispered,

"When I started this journey on that Ganeshotsav, I never imagined a day would come when so many engineers and experts would work together to fulfill my dream."

Savitri smiled, resting her hand on his shoulder.

"That's because your dream was never just yours. It was for the entire village. Yes, it started with a hope to bring back Advait... but you gave it your all, selflessly—for everyone."

Nilkanth gently held Savitri in his arms and led her inside. That night felt unlike any other in recent years—softer, fuller, and steeped in quiet triumph. As he lay down, his mind wandered through every twist and turn of the journey.

Eventually, sleep embraced him, and he drifted into dreams, reliving the moments of struggle and hope.

But the next morning arrived with an unexpected stir.

A sudden commotion outside woke them both. Nilkanth blinked at the wall clock—7:00 a.m. Savitri rubbed her eyes and shuffled to the window. What she saw left her stunned.

"Oh my goodness," she gasped under her breath. "Look… look at this! So many vehicles… TV channels, press reporters—what's happening?"

Down below, at least four or five media vans lined up in front of their house, cameras and microphones already being set up. Just as she turned back to call Nilkanth, his phone rang.

He picked up the call with a half-sleepy voice, his heart suddenly racing. It was Madam Lalitha.

"Nilkanthji," she said cheerfully, "the Honourable Minister for Water Supply and Irrigation is arriving at your home sharp at 11 a.m. Please be ready—and ask your boys to be present too. This is a proud day for all of us!"

Nilkanth stammered, overwhelmed:
"Madam… this wasn't necessary. I'm just a simple idol-maker in a forgotten village. I only did what felt like my duty…"

Lalitha's voice softened, yet stayed firm:
"We'll talk more when I arrive. I'll be there within the hour. Till then, there may be some interviews, but don't

worry—they won't begin until I and my entire geological team are present. Just be yourself. Don't hesitate."

The line went silent.

Nilkanth sat down at the edge of the bed, phone still in hand, eyes wide with disbelief. His body was still, but his mind was spinning.

Savitri quietly sat beside him, gently running her fingers through his graying hair. Her voice trembled with emotion but carried a calming strength:

"Ajoba… you deserve every bit of this. Accept it as Bappa's blessing. This is not just about Nilkanth Jadav, the man. This is about the faith you carried, the love you poured into the soil. Bappa only used your hands—this miracle was his."

Nilkanth turned toward her, eyes moist, lips quivering. He embraced her tightly, whispering,

"Thank you… for every word I needed to hear. Yes… it was never me. It was always Bappa. I was just a trustee of his will."

And in that silent, sacred moment, gratitude flowed as freely as the water they had unearthed.

Savitri rushed to the kitchen, her heart pounding with excitement and nervousness. She quickly brewed a pot of tea, and the couple sat down for a hasty sip, exchanging glances filled with anticipation. Nilkanth barely finished his cup before darting off to bathe. In the meantime, Savitri prepared a simple breakfast—poha—and carefully set aside extra portions for the four boys and Madam Lalitha, should they wish to join.

By 8:30, all four boys arrived, neatly dressed in formal shirts and trousers, their eyes sparkling with pride and nerves. Nilkanth had already informed them of the media's presence, and they had come prepared.

By 9 a.m., everything was in place.

Just then, the doorbell rang. Madam Lalitha stepped in with her team, a warm but determined look on her face. She greeted Nilkanth and immediately took him aside.

"Nilkanthji," she said, "the media will try to polish your words, spin your story. Please—speak the truth, as it is. Don't let them edit your soul. This story isn't just about water—it's about faith, courage, and relentless grit."

Nilkanth nodded earnestly, absorbing every word.

Within moments, cameras began rolling. Several channels started airing live interviews from the front yard, focusing their lenses on the modest home of the man who had changed the fate of a village.

Then, at exactly 11 a.m., a wave of security swept across the area. Police personnel and a few army officials secured the perimeter, signaling the imminent arrival of the Minister.

Soon, a black SUV pulled in, and out stepped the Honourable Minister of Water Supply and Irrigation, flanked by officers and media personnel.

Nilkanth and the boys greeted him at the gate with folded hands, bouquets, and a handmade garland strung together by Savitri the previous night. The Minister accepted it graciously and turned to Nilkanth with a wide smile.

"Nilkanthji," he said, "I am here today not just to congratulate you, but to honor you. You and your young team have accomplished something historic—unprecedented in our state's records. The Chief Minister himself sends his admiration and will visit you soon. Today, we are here to witness the beginning of a new era for this village."

He turned to Lalitha and added,
"Shall we proceed, Madam? But let Nilkanthji lead us. This day belongs to him."

A hush of awe and reverence followed as Nilkanth—humble, overwhelmed, and deeply moved—stepped forward to guide them all toward the heart of the miracle: the water pump that would soon quench the thirst of an entire village.

As the entire entourage, led by the Minister, approached the well shaft, Nilkanth gently stepped forward and requested, "Sir, for safety, I must insist that no more than six people enter the shaft at once—any more might cause air suffocation." The Minister nodded in agreement.

Nilkanth selected Madam Lalitha, the Minister's bodyguard, a cameraman, and young Prakash to accompany him. Together, they descended the carefully carved stone steps, each turn lit by strategically placed LED lights.

The Minister was visibly amazed. With every step, his astonishment deepened—marveling at the ingenuity behind the shaft's construction: the natural slope, the arched boat-like reinforcements, and the minimal cost solutions that spoke volumes about practical brilliance. The cameraman captured each expression, each word of praise the Minister offered to Nilkanth and his young team.

Finally, they reached the heart of the shaft—a heavy-duty pressure pump gleamed at the end, perfectly installed and connected to the village's underground pipeline network. Beside it stood a compact switch panel displaying sensor signals for every connected household.

Nilkanth and the operator gave a brief demonstration of the setup, and just then, a signal crackled over the walkie-talkie: "All terminals ready."

The operator turned to the Minister, gesturing.
"Sir, the honor is yours. Please initiate the supply."

The Minister smiled and pressed the button.

Within moments, green signals blinked rapidly across the panel—one after another. Outside, cheers erupted as the villagers watched indicators confirming water had reached at least 25 homes.

Inside the shaft, applause filled the narrow space—echoing like a hymn of victory.

That moment marked not just the flow of water, but a historic milestone, carved by the hands of a humble idol-maker and four relentless boys.

The Minister, accompanied by Madam Lalitha, Nilkanth, and Prakash, emerged from the well shaft to a sea of flashing cameras and eager reporters. The media immediately surged forward, requesting the Minister's opinion on the groundbreaking achievement. With a warm smile and steady voice, the Minister began praising Nilkanth—calling him "a rare visionary whose hands shaped not only idols but the destiny of an entire village."

Nilkanth stood humbly to one side, flanked by his four students—Suresh, Mohan, Prashant, and Pankaj. While the boys beamed with pride, Nilkanth looked visibly shy, overwhelmed by the honor. For a man used to clay and silence, standing before a national audience, being lauded by a cabinet minister, was almost too much to bear.

The entire event was being broadcast live across leading news channels, national television, and radio stations. Across the state and beyond, people watched the quiet triumph of an ordinary man who dared to believe.

Then came the announcement.

The Minister declared an official award of Rupees 25 lakhs from the government in recognition of Nilkanth's contribution to rural development. A ceremonial shawl was draped around Nilkanth's shoulders and all four boys, and a garland of fresh marigolds adorned to Nilkanth and all four boys. Followed by applauds by the cheering crowd. Nilkanth was handed a cheque and a letter of appreciation signed personally by the Chief Minister where name of Nilkanth and all four boys were mentioned in golden ink.

Savitri, standing in the crowd, could barely hold back her tears. Seeing her husband being celebrated on such a grand scale was a moment she had never dared to imagine.

Noticing her, Nilkanth stepped down from the dais and gently brought her forward, saying, "This is the woman who stood by me when no one did." The Minister, moved by her quiet strength, honored Savitri with a beautiful sari and a ceremonial shawl.

That moment—broadcast into homes far and wide—brought tears to thousands. In a world full of noise, it was the story of one humble man, his devoted wife, and four determined boys who dared to dig through stone and fate, and bring water—hope—back to their village.

The same villagers who once ignored Nilkanth's silent sacrifices and brushed aside Savitri's quiet strength now came running—bearing sweets, garlands, and words of praise. Their eyes glistened with tears, their voices trembling with gratitude. The air was filled with chants, embraces, and unspoken apologies as they surrounded the couple who had, without fanfare, gifted the village its greatest blessing.

Madam Lalitha and her team escorted the Minister to the guesthouse for a formal lunch and also invited Nilkanth and Savitri and boys. But Savitri in turn invited them and said-"Madam We will be grateful if Minister Sir and you all have lunch with us. As I have made much of the arrangement only a half an hour will be enough for me. Lalitha replied-"Nilkanthji and Savitriji the lunch arrangements were already done so we could not skip we appreciate your invitation, I will definitely come for lunch someday soon as the Minister had ordered to install a reservoir nearby." Savitri and Nilkanth thanked her with heartfelt gratitude and appreciated her endeavour, still dazed by the emotional storm that had swept through his humble life. As Lalitha boarded her car she smiled and said- "Ghanshyam had been suspended for an indefinite period Nilkanthji, we are thankful to Prashant for helping us clear the debris."

Savitri, ever the quiet anchor, walked back into the kitchen to serve lunch to Nilkanth and the boys. Just then, her phone rang. She answered, her hands still trembling. On the other end, she heard two voices—choked with tears. It was Vinayak and Jayashree.

"Aai..." Vinayak began, his voice breaking, "Why didn't you or Baba ever tell us about any of this? Today our friends called, saying Baba was on TV—being honored by the Minister. We didn't know... Are we so distant now... so alien to you both?"

Savitri froze. The ladle dropped from her hand. Tears poured down her face, her chest heaving with years of suppressed sorrow.

Vinayak continued, his voice thick, "Aai, I'm applying for a transfer today. We're coming back—for good. With Advait. This distance... this silence... it's over."

Savitri couldn't hold it any longer. A cry escaped her lips—a cry that carried the pain of every Ganesh Chaturthi without her son, every dinner where she set a plate but never served it. Her voice trembled as she whispered, "Come back, beta... We've waited long enough. We're still waiting."

Then Jayashree spoke, her voice soft and warm, "Aai… let Baba be surprised. Advait knows now. He knows his grandfather is no ordinary man—he's the one who can breathe life into Ganpati… and into an entire village. He made water flow where there was none. He did the impossible, Aai."

She paused, and then added, "My parents are coming with us. They want to meet the man who changed not just a village, but all of us."

Savitri wiped her tears with the edge of her sari, her heart overflowing. Through her tears, she smiled and said, "Don't worry, beta… our hearts are bigger than any mansion. There is space for all of you. Always."

And as she hung up the call, she looked toward the sky from the window, whispering her thanks to Bappa. For bringing water to her village. For bringing her family back home.

Nilkanth walked into the kitchen, his face still glowing from the day's whirlwind of emotions. He gently called out,

"My sweetheart, we're all hungry… can we get some lunch?"

Savitri, still lost in the afterglow of the phone call, turned to him with tears lingering in her eyes. She quickly wiped them away and smiled,

"Yes… I'm coming. You all sit at the table. It's ready."

Noticing the glisten in her eyes, Nilkanth stepped closer and whispered softly,

"Were you crying?"

Then, with a tender smile, he added,

"Let's thank Bappa. He's taken care of everything—our dreams, our village, even our finances. Now it's our turn to get back to work… Ganeshotsav is just a few weeks away. Let's return to the workshop. If Bappa has provided for us, we must now prepare to welcome him with all our heart."

That evening, as the golden light of dusk poured gently over the courtyard, Nilkanth sat on the verandah, a cup of tea warming his palms. His eyes wandered to the vibrant bouquets placed in the old brass vase—blooms so exotic, their names were unfamiliar. He suddenly chuckled to himself, the sound full of disbelief.

Savitri, setting down her own cup, looked at him and teased,

"What's gotten into you? These honors have truly made you mad. I've never seen you like this."

Nilkanth smiled, still gazing at the flowers.

"Look at them, Savitri. These are the rarest flowers I've ever seen… decorating my tea table."

He paused, then added, his voice softening,

"Yet, the ones I waited for the most… my own son, his wife, my little Advait… haven't even called. Not a word."

Savitri's smile faded. Her heart clenched at the secret she held close. She turned her face away and replied in a carefully neutral tone,

"Maybe they're just busy… you know how life is. I'm sure they'll call soon. Do you… do you really miss them that much?"

Nilkanth's gaze dropped to his cup. The steam blurred his eyes, but not enough to hide the tears that began to form. His voice came out strained,

"He's my son, Savitri. My only son. And he's the father of my only grandson… Don't I have the right to miss them?"

Savitri couldn't hold back any longer. She placed her hand gently on his shoulder and leaned closer, her voice trembling,

"He will call. I promise you, he will. Bappa has already given us so much… he won't ignore your prayers. Even the ache of a father's heart—he will hear that too."

Nilkanth nodded slowly, holding her hand in his. The silence between them was no longer empty—it was filled with hope.

Night descended softly over the village, yet a quiet heaviness lingered in the air—an ache that clung to the walls of the old house, echoing the wordless sorrow of a father's longing. Savitri, though comforted by the day's honors and her husband's joy, couldn't shake the restlessness stirring within her. Watching Nilkanth's eyes, she saw not pride, but a yearning for something more precious than accolades—a yearning only a son's return could fulfill.

Then came the dawn,

As the first light kissed the sea on the horizon, painting the sky in hues of gold and rose, a new day arrived—one that had long waited in silence to reveal its surprise.

Nilkanth had just finished freshening up, and Savitri was on her way to bring him tea when the doorbell rang. Before she could reach the handle, a child's excited shriek pierced the air. Nilkanth opened the door, confused… and then, time stopped.

There stood Vinayak, his eyes filled with tears, rushing to fall at the feet of his father. Behind him, Jayashree, cradling little Advait, gently lowered her head in reverence. She placed the boy in Vinayak's arms and bent to touch the feet of Nilkanth and Savitri.

Nilkanth stood frozen—spellbound, breathless, as tears poured down his cheeks without shame.

The little one, Advait, looked on silently, his curious eyes scanning the face he had so often drawn in his sketchbook. Jayashree knelt beside him and said softly:

"Betu… here's your Ajoba. The one you've always wanted to meet."

Advait blinked once… then smiled, a slow, shy smile that made the world pause.

He tilted his head and asked in a gentle Marathi lilt:

"Ajoba… Ganpati ata mala bhetayla yeyil ka?"

(Grandfather, will Ganpati come to meet me now?)

Nilkanth broke down completely, sobbing with joy. He swept Advait into his arms and held him tightly, as though trying to erase the ache of three long, silent years in one embrace.

In that sacred moment, pain turned into light. Time folded, and every wound of separation vanished.

Shankar and Deepa entered quietly behind them, holding a bouquet. Shankar placed it in Nilkanth's hands and said, his voice choked,

"We're proud of you, Dada. Truly proud."

Deepa stepped forward hesitantly.

"Dada… I know I've wronged you. I'm ashamed of how I behaved. Please forgive me."

Nilkanth shook his head gently and said,

"Bahini… I'd already forgotten. Don't remind me of what's past. Let's hold on only to what's come home."

Jayashree moved to take Advait back, but the boy clung to Nilkanth's lap and declared,

"Aai! I will hear stories only from Ajoba now."

Savitri, beaming through tears, welcomed them all in. She brought out hot tea and snacks, urging everyone to rest after their long journey. Laughter returned to the home, now alive with the sounds of three generations under one roof.

As Nilkanth played with Advait on the floor, Vinayak approached him and placed a hand on his father's shoulder.

"Baba… I've applied for a transfer to the government school here. Before Ganeshotsav begins, I'll be home—forever."

Nilkanth turned to Savitri, unable to contain his joy.

"Have you heard what Vinayak just said? He's coming back—forever!"

Savitri laughed brightly, her eyes twinkling.

"Yes, Sir! I've known since yesterday. This whole surprise… we planned it after your award ceremony."

Nilkanth raised an eyebrow, mock-scowling.

"So, all of you were enjoying my pain while I sat mourning them yesterday?"

Jayashree giggled and said,

"Baba, if we had told you beforehand, we wouldn't have seen you so happy today. Advait's arrival had to be a miracle… like the water you brought to this village."

Still holding his grandson close, Nilkanth turned to the little one and said,

"Your Aai, Baba, and Ajji are all very naughty. But now that you're here, let's enjoy our first day together at the sea."

Advait clapped with joy, placing his tiny palm on his own head, imitating a blessing.

Moments later, Nilkanth hoisted him onto his shoulders, his smile brighter than the morning sun.

"Vinayak," he called out, "if you're coming, join me and my Natu for a walk by the shore."

Vinayak followed, camera in hand, capturing frame after frame of a love so divine it could melt the hardest heart—the love between an Ajoba and his Natu.

As they passed the village square, Nilkanth's old friends came rushing out.

"Nilkanth! So proud of you!"

He waved at them and grinned,

"Not now! My Natu and I are busy. We'll chat later!"

The sun climbed higher as laughter and sea breeze danced together.

www.ingramcontent.com/pod-product-compliance
Ingram Content Group UK Ltd.
Pitfield, Milton Keynes, MK11 3LW, UK
UKHW041345190726
13845UKWH00026B/430

9 788199 203822